Ashley felt trapped. Cornered.

It was a struggle to remain still and meet Sebastian's gaze.

"What do you want from me?"

"Two weeks in my bed."

Her skin went hot and her mouth dropped open. "I wouldn't stay in your bed for two more minutes let alone—"

"Make it three," he said coldly.

Her eyes widened. "You..." she bit out.

"And now it's four," he said with no emotion. "Do you want to make it five weeks?"

A month with Sebastian? The wall she had painstakingly built around herself had shattered after one night with him. What would happen to her after four weeks in his bed?

"How long do I have before I give you my decision?"

He moved closer, his mouth above hers. She felt his warm breath waft over her skin. "You have to give it to me now. Take it or leave it," he said.

Susanna Carr

—

A Deal with Benefits

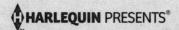

Recycling programs
for this product may
not exist in your area.

ISBN-13: 978-0-373-13214-0

A DEAL WITH BENEFITS

First North American Publication 2014

Copyright © 2014 by Susanna Carr

HARLEQUIN®
www.Harlequin.com

Printed in U.S.A.

All about the author...
Susanna Carr

SUSANNA CARR has been an avid romance reader since she read her first Harlequin Presents® book at the age of ten. Although romance novels were not allowed in her home, she always managed to sneak one in from the local library or from her twin sister's secret stash.

After attending college and receiving a degree in English Literature, Susanna pursued a romance writing career. She has written sexy contemporary romances for several publishers and her work has been honored with awards for contemporary and sensual romance.

Susanna Carr lives in the Pacific Northwest with her family. When she isn't writing, Susanna enjoys reading romance and connecting with readers online. Visit her website at susannacarr.com.

Other titles by Susanna Carr available in ebook:

HER SHAMEFUL SECRET
JAZAAR'S TARNISHED JEWEL

To my editor, Carly Byrne, with thanks

PROLOGUE

"Our guest is early, Miss Ashley. Ooh, that boat is sweet," Clea, the housekeeper, said and gave a squeal of laughter that rang through the hall. "You should see Louis running down the dock to get a closer look."

"It must be quite a boat," Ashley said. Clea's husband didn't move fast. No one did on Inez Key. Their families had been here for generations and they followed the gentle rhythm of island life.

Ashley took a step outside and stared at the scarlet red boat. The sharp and dramatic lines seemed obscenely aggressive against the lazy waves of the ocean. The boat said a lot about the owner. Loud and attention seeking. She squinted and noticed that there was only one person on the boat. "Damn," she muttered. "He's single."

Clea patted Ashley's bare arm. "I'm sure he won't require that much work."

Ashley rolled her eyes. "Single guests are the worst. They expect to be entertained."

"I can meet him while you change into a dress," Clea said as she headed down the hill to the dock.

Ashley followed her. "No, thanks. I'm not dressing up for paying guests anymore. Not after that basketball player thought I was included in the weekend package."

Clea gestured at Ashley. "And what is this man going to think when he sees you dressed like that?"

Ashley looked down at the bright yellow tank top that didn't quite reach the frayed cutoff shorts. Her worn sandals were so old they clung lovingly to her feet and her long hair was gathered up in a messy ponytail. She only wore makeup or jewelry for a special occasion. A man did not fall into that category. "That we aren't formal around here."

Clea clucked her tongue and stared at Ashley's long brown legs. "You don't know much about men, do you?"

"I've learned more than I ever wish to know," Ashley said. She'd got her education whenever her father had been around during the tennis off-season. What she didn't discover from Donald Jones, she had learned from his entourage.

She had finally used all that knowledge to secure a generous loan from Raymond Casillas. It had been a huge risk. She didn't trust the aging playboy and knew he was going to find a way to have her repay him with sex. That wasn't going to happen.

Unfortunately, she was behind on her loan payment and she couldn't miss another month. Ashley shuddered, the icy-cold fear trickling down her spine as she considered the consequences. Just a few more rich celebrities seeking privacy on her island—okay, quite a few more—and she would be free of the threat.

Ashley walked down the hill with renewed determination. She strode along the sturdy wood dock, blocking the bright sun with her hand as she took a closer look at her guest, Sebastian Esteban.

The man stood on the deck like a conquering hero waiting to be swarmed by the grateful natives. Her heart started to pound against her chest. She noticed the thick dark hair ruffling slightly in the wind and the T-shirt stretched against his broad chest. His powerful legs were encased in faded jeans. She felt an unfamiliar pull low in her belly as she stared at the gorgeous stranger.

"Huh," Clea said as she walked alongside Ashley. "There's something familiar about that man."

"Is he famous? An actor?" Ashley immediately dismissed that idea. While his stunning good looks would make Hollywood lay down the red carpet for him, she sensed Sebastian Esteban wasn't the kind who would trade on his harsh, masculine features. The blade of his nose and the slash of his mouth suggested aristocracy, but the high, slanted cheekbones and the thrust of his angular jaw indicated that he fought for every inch of his territory.

"Can't say for sure," Clea muttered. "I feel like I've seen him before."

It didn't matter what he did for a living, she decided. She wasn't going to be starstruck. Ashley had intentionally cut herself off from the world when her parents died five years ago. She would probably recognize a few superstars, but she didn't keep up with the current celebrities. Yet she didn't think she could tolerate another famous person who thought basic manners applied to everyone else and not them.

"Mr. Esteban?" Ashley asked as she reached out her hand. She looked up and their gazes clashed and held. Her safe little existence went completely still as the beat of her heart pounded in her ears. Anticipation rushed through her as Sebastian touched her hand. When his large fingers enclosed hers, her world shifted. She saw the glow of interest in his dark eyes as the energy, wild and violent, ripped through her.

Ashley wanted to jerk back, but the stranger held her fingers captive. Her muscles clenched as every instinct told her to hide. But she couldn't move. She was frozen as the dark, swirling emotions threatened to pull her under.

"Please, call me Sebastian."

She shivered at the sound of his rough, deep voice. "I'm Ashley," she said. It was difficult to push the words out of her tight throat. "Welcome to Inez Key. I hope you will enjoy your visit."

Something hot and wicked flickered in his eyes before he released her hand. "Thank you, I will."

As she stiffly introduced Clea and Louis, she reluctantly noticed how Sebastian towered over her, his broad shoulders blocking out the sun. She could feel his masculine power coming off him in waves.

She covertly watched him as he refused Louis's assistance and tossed his backpack over his shoulder. Who was this man? He was wealthy enough to own that boat, but he didn't wear designer clothes. He had no entourage or tower of luggage, but he could afford to stay at her home for an exclusive weekend.

"You'll stay here in the main house," Clea said as they escorted him up the hill toward the white mansion.

Sebastian stood for a moment as he studied the plantation home. His expression was blank and his eyes were hooded, but she felt an explosive tension emanating from him.

Ashley wondered what he thought about her home. The guests were always in awe of the antebellum architecture. They saw the clean lines and graceful symmetry, the massive columns that stretched from the ground to the black rooftop and surrounded every side of the house. The balconies hinted of an elegant world long forgotten and one could almost ignore that the large black window shutters were for protection from the elements instead of decoration.

But no one noticed that her home was falling apart. There was only so much that a slap of paint, a carefully angled table or a fresh bouquet of flowers could hide. The antique furniture, the artwork, anything of value, had been sold years ago.

As they walked into the grand hall, she dimly heard Clea offer refreshments. Ashley glanced around and hoped she had not overlooked anything. She wanted Sebastian Esteban to notice the curving staircase and how the sunlight caught the crystal chandelier instead of the faded wallpaper. Yet the way he quietly studied the room, she sensed that he saw everything.

Ashley stifled a gasp when she felt Clea jab her bony elbow in her ribs. "Miss Ashley, why don't you show Mr. Sebastian his room while I get the drinks?"

She gritted her teeth. "Of course. This way, please."

Ashley bent her head as she approached the stairs. She didn't want to be alone with this man. She wasn't afraid of Sebastian Esteban, but she was uncomfortable with her reaction. This wasn't like her.

Ashley's skin tingled as she climbed the stairs ahead of Sebastian. Her cutoff shorts felt small as she felt his heated gaze on her bare legs. She should have listened to Clea and worn a dress that covered every inch of skin.

But she immediately dismissed that idea. She wanted to hide, but at the same time she wanted Sebastian to notice her. Her chest rose and fell as she quickened her step. Ashley wished she could ignore the fast and furious attraction. So what if she found Sebastian sexy? Any woman would find him desirable.

Ashley didn't look at Sebastian as she flung open the door to the master suite and gestured for him to enter. "This is your room," she announced. "The walk-in closet and bathroom is through that door."

He strode to the center of the room and Ashley knew he wouldn't find fault in his accommodations here. It was the largest room and offered a magnificent view. She had placed the best furniture in the sitting area. The four-poster bed was carved mahogany and was big enough for him to lie in the center with his arms stretched out.

Ashley closed her eyes as the unwelcoming heat flushed through her skin. Why did she have to think of that? She wanted to purge the idea of him on the bed, as he lay on the rumpled sheets, naked and gleaming with sweat. She imagined his lean and muscular arms extended as if he was waiting for her. Welcoming her.

"Am I kicking you out of your bed?" Sebastian asked.

"What?" she asked hoarsely. The vision of her curled up next to him on the four-poster bed bloomed in her mind. She shook her head to dispel it. "No, I don't stay here."

"Why not?" he asked as he tossed his backpack on the bed. The bag looked out of place against the vintage handmade quilt. "It's the master suite, isn't it?"

"Yes." She nervously darted the tip of her tongue along her dry lips. She couldn't explain it to him. That this room, this bed, had been the center stage for her parents' destructive relationship. The affair between her father, Donald Jones, and her mother, his longtime mistress Linda Valdez had been fueled with jealousy, infidelities and sexual obsession. She didn't want the added reminder. "Well, if you need anything, please let me know," she said as she slowly made her way to the door.

He tore his gaze away from the ocean view and Ashley saw the shadows in his eyes. It was more than sadness. It was grief. Loss. Anger. Sebastian blinked and the shadows suddenly disappeared.

Sebastian silently nodded and walked to the door with her. He guided her through the threshold by placing his hand on the small of her back. His fingers brushed her bare skin and her muscles clenched as her skin tightened. He dropped his hand, but she still felt the blood strumming through her veins.

Ashley took a deep breath and hurried away from Sebastian, refusing to look back. She was scared to explore these feelings. She was not used to being tempted while she stayed on Inez Key and this was going to be a challenge. She had hidden away for years, purposely disconnected from the world and was quiet and contained. None of the guests who came to her house interested her, but this man...this man reminded her of what she was missing.

And she wasn't sure she wanted to hide anymore....

CHAPTER ONE

One month later

"Sir? There's a woman here who wishes to speak with you."

Sebastian Cruz didn't look up as he continued to sign papers. "Send her away." He didn't tolerate any kind of interruption while he was at work. It was probably a former lover who mistakenly thought the element of surprise and drama would gain his attention. His employees were experienced in handling the situation and he wondered how the woman had managed to get into the executive suite in the first place.

"She insists on seeing you and hasn't left the reception area all day," his assistant continued, this time with a hint of sympathy for the uninvited guest. "She says it's urgent."

They all said that, Sebastian decided as he scanned another letter before he signed it. It annoyed him rather than made him feel curious or flattered. He didn't understand why these sophisticated women would stage public tantrums when the relationship was clearly over. "Have security remove her from the premises."

The younger man cleared his throat and nervously adjusted his tie. "I had considered that, but she says you have something of hers. She wouldn't tell me what it was because it was a private matter. She's here to get it back."

That was impossible. Sebastian frowned as he scrawled his name on another document. He wasn't sentimental. He didn't keep mementos or trophies. "Did you find out her name?"

His assistant squirmed from the censure of his icy tone. "Jones," he said hurriedly. "Ashley Jones."

Sebastian went still as he held the pen in midair. He stared at the heavy paper, the words a blur, as memories of Ashley Jones crashed through him. He remembered her soft brown hair cascading down her bare shoulders. Her wild energy and her earthy laugh. His body clenched, excitement pulsing through his veins, as he thought about her sun-kissed skin and wide pink mouth.

That woman had haunted his dreams for the past month. He had tried to purge Ashley from his mind, distracting himself with work and women, but he couldn't forget her uninhibited response. Or her haughty rejection.

Sebastian remembered that morning vividly. She had still been naked in bed when she had told him she wasn't interested in anything more than a one-night stand. She had shared more than her body that night, but now he wasn't good enough to breathe her rarefied air. Her lips had been reddened from his kisses, but she wouldn't deign to look him in the eye.

Ashley had no idea that he was the most sought-after

bachelor in Miami. A billionaire with incredible influence. Women of power, wealth and royalty chased after him. He had shed the stench of the ghetto years ago and now belonged to the glittery world of high society. But she had dismissed him as if she was a princess that belonged in an ivory-white tower and he still belonged in the filthy streets. Who did she think she was? Ashley had never lifted a finger for the lifestyle she enjoyed, while he continued to fight for the empire he'd created with his bare hands.

"I think she's the daughter of that tennis legend," his assistant continued in a scandalized whisper. "You know, the murder-suicide. It was big news a few years ago."

Donald Jones. Sebastian's nostrils flared as he forced back the rising hot anger. He knew all about the tennis player and his family. He had made a point of learning everything about Ashley.

There had been a few surprises when he had met her, but his first impression had been correct. She was a spoiled heiress who lived in paradise. She didn't know the meaning of scraping by, suffering or surviving. For a woman like Ashley Jones, the world catered to her.

Until now. Sebastian narrowed his eyes as an idea formed. Anticipation beat hard in his chest as he considered the possibilities. He knew why she was here. She wanted to find out how he'd got her precious island and how she could get it back.

His mouth twisted as he imagined his revenge. She wouldn't be so quick to dismiss him now that he had something she wanted. Now was his chance to watch her bow down and lose that superior tone. Sebastian wanted to turn the tables and strip this woman of her pride and status. Take her to bed for one night, indulge in the exquisite pleasure that would make the most cynical lover believe in destiny, and then discard her.

"Please send her in," Sebastian said coldly as the call of the hunt roared in his blood, "and then you may leave for the day."

Ashley sat on the edge of the pearl-white leather chair as she watched the sun set over the Miami skyline. She felt a pang of homesickness as she saw how the tall buildings pierced the coral and dusky pink streaks in the sky. She felt uncomfortable surrounded by steel and glass, noise and people. She missed sitting alone in her favorite spot in the cove of her island and watching the sun dip past the endless turquoise ocean.

She may never see it again. Fear squeezed her heart, and her fingers pinched her white clutch purse. Bile churned in her stomach as she remembered the eviction letter. She still felt the same agonizing horror when she had discovered a Sebastian Cruz had bought her loan and now owned her family island because she'd missed two payments.

Ashley pressed her lips together and prayed that she could meet Mr. Cruz and come to an understanding. Get her island back immediately. What was she going to do if she couldn't get the man to see reason?

She couldn't think this way. Ashley exhaled slowly, wishing the panic that banded her chest would dissolve.

Defeat was not an option. This was her last chance, but she was going to find a way to get back her family home.

Ashley glanced around the waiting room, noticing that it was quieter now that most of the office workers had gone for the day. It didn't make the space any less intimidating. She almost hadn't stepped into the building when she noticed the towering height and the aggressive sleek lines. It had taken more courage than she'd care to admit to stay seated on the chair throughout the day, feeling small and invisible, as she watched the employees attack the day with ruthless energy.

Her head jerked when she heard purposeful footsteps echo against the polished black floor. The tall man in the designer suit and prestigious school tie she'd spoken with earlier approached her. "Miss Jones? Mr. Cruz can see you now."

Ashley nodded as her throat tightened with anxiety. Her hands went suddenly cold as she rose from the seat. She felt uncoordinated, her legs stiff and her borrowed heels heavy, as she followed the man in the suit.

You can fix this, she reminded herself fiercely as she nervously smoothed her hand over her hair. It had taken ages to coax her wild mane into a tight bun and she felt as if the waves were threatening to break free.

As she tried to keep up with the man who was undoubtedly an assistant, she tried not to notice the imposing features of the stark and colorless corridor. She didn't know how this Sebastian Cruz had got Inez Key, but she knew it had to be a mistake. She couldn't imagine why someone with this amount of wealth would want a run-down island.

Ashley glanced at the assistant. She was tempted to ask about Sebastian Cruz, but she sensed the man wouldn't reveal much. She regretted not researching the man who owned Cruz Conglomerate. If the executive suite indicated anything, she suspected Sebastian Cruz was an older, formal gentleman who valued propriety and status.

Ashley tugged at the vintage white dress that had once belonged to her mother. She was glad she'd made the choice to wear it. It was outdated and restricting but she knew she looked sweet and demure.

Now, if only she could remember to speak like a lady. Ashley paused at the grand black doors to Mr. Cruz's office. Everything went into slow motion as she watched the assistant knock and open the door. *Just watch your mouth.* Ashley swiped the tip of her tongue along her dry lips. She knew more than anyone how one reckless word could ruin everything....

Ashley barely heard the assistant's introduction over the sound of her heart pounding in her ears. She sensed the magnitude of the room but controlled the impulse of looking around. She placed a polite smile on her lips, stretched out her hand and froze when she saw Sebastian Cruz.

"You!" she blurted out as she instinctively snatched her hand back. Standing before her was the one man she'd hoped she'd never meet again. *This* was Sebastian Cruz? The man had turned her world upside down a month ago, had torn down all of her defenses and introduced her to a world of pleasure and promise.

Ashley gasped for her next breath as her body went rigid, primed to flee. What was going on? This could not be Sebastian Cruz. It was Sebastian *Esteban*. The name was burned into her mind forever. A woman never forgot her first lover.

But this man didn't look anything like the mysterious guest who had arrived for a weekend getaway on Inez Key a month ago. The faded jeans and knowing smile were replaced with a severe suit and a stern mouth. Her gaze traveled from his short black hair to his large brown eyes and the hard thrust of his chin. He was attractive but forbidding. Menacing.

Sebastian's raw power was barely concealed underneath the tailored lines of his black suit. His lean and muscular build hinted that he was sleek, swift and that he moved with stealth. This man could fight hard and dirty.

He smiled and a sense of unease trickled down Ashley's spine. This time his smile didn't make her heart give a slow tumble. His sharp white teeth made her think of a cold-blooded animal tearing apart his quarry.

Feeling a little shaky, Ashley took a step back. Sebastian was stunning, but her memories had muted the brutal power and raw masculinity he possessed.

"Ashley," he said silkily and gestured at the chair in front of his desk. He didn't look surprised to see her. "Please sit down."

"What are you doing here?" she asked as conflicting

emotions swirled ferociously inside her. She felt dizzy. Vulnerable. She wanted to sit down and curl into a protective ball but she couldn't give the man any advantage. "I don't understand. He called you Mr. Cruz."

"That is my name," he said as he sat down behind his desk.

"Since when?" She winced when her voice rose. Ashley tried desperately to hold back. "You introduced yourself to me as Sebastian Esteban."

"That is part of my name. Esteban is my mother's family name." His dark eyes were intent as he watched her closely. As if that name should mean something to her. "I am Sebastian Esteban Cruz."

That was his excuse? She stared at him, waiting for more. Instead, he sat in his chair that was as big as a throne and watched her with an air of impatience. He wasn't going to apologize for anything.

"Why did you lie to me? Is that part of your routine?" A woman only had to look at Sebastian Cruz and know he was a heartbreaker. She thought she could remain unscathed by limiting their encounter to a one-night stand. She had been wrong.

But she hadn't been thinking during that sensual weekend, she thought as regret pricked at her. Instead, she had followed a primal call and fallen into Sebastian's bed.

She had known better. Expected more from herself. After being raised by a philandering father, Ashley had recognized the signs of Sebastian's tried-and-true routine. She should have remembered the devastation that immediately followed the promise of paradise.

"When a wealthy person is interested in buying property, it's in their best interest not to reveal who they are," he said unrepentantly. "Otherwise the sale price goes up."

"Inez Key wasn't for sale," she said hoarsely as the anger whipped through her. Now she understood why he'd chosen to visit her island. He had intended to steal her family home from the beginning!

"So you kept saying." He gave a dismissive shrug. "I had approached you through several of my representatives, but I kept getting the same answer. The offered price was extremely generous. I made a personal visit in the hopes that I could convince you to sell."

She had thought it was strange that a man like Sebastian had arrived at her island for rest and relaxation. He was the kind of man who thrived on challenges and conquering uncharted territory. "Instead, you stole it from me," she whispered as her stomach churned. "This is all making sense."

"I didn't steal it," he corrected her. "You missed the deadline to repay the loan. Inez Key is mine."

Ashley didn't like the triumph she heard in his voice. She clenched her purse tighter as she choked back the fury. "That loan is none of your business! It was a private agreement between Raymond Casillas and me."

"And I bought the loan from Casillas. You shouldn't have put up your island as collateral." He mockingly clucked his tongue and shook his head at her poor judgment.

"It not like I had a lot of choices," she pointed out fiercely. How dare this man question her decision? Her father's finances had been a shambles when he died. Sebastian had no idea what she'd had to do, what she'd had to sacrifice, to keep Inez Key. "It was the only thing I have of value."

He tilted his head and captured her gaze. "Was it?" he asked softly.

Ashley stiffened as she sensed the danger lurking beneath that question. How much did this man know? She needed to take control of this meeting. Her legs shook and she felt jittery, but she forced herself to remain standing. "Inez Key suffered a lot of damage during the hurricane, and the insurance wouldn't pay for all of it."

He shrugged. "I don't care how you got into debt."

She wanted to claw at his bored expression. Ashley curled her fingers into her palms as she felt her temper flare dangerously. "I didn't make an agreement with you," she said roughly. "I had a payment plan with Raymond."

"Which you couldn't pay," he said. "You took a gamble and you lost."

Ashley gritted her teeth. It was true and she couldn't deny it. She had taken many risks when she'd accepted the loan. She'd had difficulty finding the money to repay, but she couldn't let it end here. She had to get Inez Key back.

"Raymond understood why I was having trouble making the payments," she said, her voice shaking as emotions ran wild inside her. "He was giving me more time since he had been best friends with my father."

"I'm sure he was the epitome of understanding and compassion. But it was smart of you to keep it out of the banking system." He wagged his finger at her. "I would have found out about it earlier."

Did he think this was funny? That this was a game? Her future was at stake here. "And then you wouldn't have had to sleep with me to get that kind of information," she retorted.

Sebastian's gaze slowly traveled down her tense body, resting briefly on her gentle curves. "That isn't why I took you to bed."

Her skin burned. She couldn't stop the fragmented memories flooding her mind. She remembered his hot masculine scent and the taste of his golden skin. Her dress felt tight as she recalled the sharp hiss between his teeth and the bite of pain when his strong fingers had tangled in her hair.

Ashley abruptly looked away. She had a tendency to remember that night at the most inconvenient moments. Her heart was pounding against her chest and her body was flushed. "You didn't have seduction in mind the moment you stepped on Inez Key," she mumbled. "I find that highly unlikely."

"I didn't know that you would indulge in pillow talk after sex," he drawled as he leaned back in his chair and steepled his long fingers together. "I certainly didn't expect you to reveal your agreement with Casillas. That was a bonus and it was impossible for me not to use that information for my benefit."

Ashley stared at Sebastian as her chest twisted painfully. How could he be so callous about that intimate moment? Didn't he realize that she never confided in anyone? But she had felt close and safe enough to tell

him her worries. She had been interested in his opinion and valued his advice. It was only in the light of
day that she realized she had been lulled into a false
sense of security.

She somehow knew that rare slip of the tongue would
come back and haunt her. He had used that moment of
weakness to his advantage. "I will not allow you to take
this island from me!"

Sebastian was unmoved by her heated declaration.
"It's too late."

"Why are you being so unreasonable?" Her voice
echoed in her ears. She lowered her hands firmly against
her sides and tried again. "Why can't you give me a second chance?"

He seemed genuinely surprised by her question. As if
she was more naive than he had given her credit. "Why
should I? Have you done anything that would suggest
you deserve a second chance?"

She saw the way his eyes darkened. There was something about his choice of words. Suspicion slithered
and coiled around her weary mind as she crossed her
arms. "Is this because I kicked you out of bed the next
morning?"

Ashley wanted to bite her tongue the moment she
spoke without thinking. She knew she had to be careful with her words. She cringed as she heard his husky
chuckle.

Sebastian's smile was a slash of white against his
dark skin. "Don't flatter yourself."

She knew she had caught him off guard when she'd

refused his offer to continue the relationship. Sebastian would never know how much the idea had both delighted and scared her. If he had seen her resolve weaken, he would have gone in for the kill. Her answer came across cold and unfeeling and she knew the rejection had stung.

To think she had felt bad about it! She had spent hours reviewing that moment and wishing she had refused more gracefully. And more than once she wished she had the courage to have accepted his offer.

But she realized that even after one glorious night, she was in danger of becoming the kind of woman she hated. A sexual creature. A woman who was driven by her emotions and needs. She had pulled away to protect herself.

"I can't help but think this is all personal," she said, glaring at him.

He arched a dark eyebrow. "How is that possible when we had not met until I arrived on Inez Key?" he murmured.

Ashley felt as if she was missing something. She knew they'd never met. One would never forget the briefest encounter with Sebastian Cruz. "You lied to me about your name, you had a hidden agenda and you seduced me. I was right to follow my instincts and get rid of you."

"And I'm right to follow my instincts and remove you from the island immediately," Sebastian said, clicking his computer keyboard as if the discussion was over.

Immediately? Panic gripped her chest. Before she'd walked in here she'd had two weeks to leave the island.

She was making this worse. "Inez Key is all I have," she said in a rush. "Without it, I have no home, no money…"

He didn't glance away from the computer screen. "That is not my concern."

She marched over to his desk and braced her hands on the edge. She would demand his attention if she had to reach over and grab him by the throat. "How can you be so cruel?" she asked in a low growl.

He lifted his gaze and held hers. "Cruel? You don't know the meaning."

She leaned forward. "I can't lose Inez Key. That is my home and my livelihood."

"Livelihood?" He scoffed at the word. "You haven't worked a day in your life. You rent out your home to wealthy people for the occasional weekend."

She let that criticism slide. She may not have a traditional job, but that didn't mean she didn't work hard to hold on to everything that was dear to her. "They pay good money for privacy. You did. What makes you think others won't?"

He reached for his pen and uncapped it. "There aren't enough rich celebrities looking for privacy to pay back your loan."

"I haven't been doing it long enough," she insisted. She needed to buy a little time. "Raymond understood that."

Sebastian shook his head. "Raymond Casillas wanted you to dig a deeper hole. He knew you were never going to be able to pay back the loan. Why do you think he offered in the first place?"

Ashley straightened and took a step away from the desk. "I don't know," she muttered. She didn't want to talk about it. Her skin felt prickly as the nausea swept through her.

"He hoped you would pay back in another way. And I think you knew that. Which is why you had requested a contract. Under most circumstances, it would have been a smart move."

"A lot of good it did me," she said under her breath. That contract now put her right in the hands of the ruthless Sebastian Cruz.

"You didn't want there to be any misunderstanding. You would offer Inez Key as your collateral, not your body." Sebastian paused. "Or your virginity."

She flushed bright red and refused to meet his gaze. "You knew?" Ashley whispered. She had done everything to conceal her inexperience. Out of pride, out of protection. She couldn't allow Sebastian to know how much advantage he had in that moment. But how did he know? How did she give herself away?

He set down the pen. "You should have told me." His tone was almost soft. Kind.

Ashley took another step back. She felt exposed. She wished she could walk right out of the office, but her unfamiliar heels felt like shackles. "I had already told you too much. And how did you know that Raymond wanted..." She swallowed roughly as her voice trailed away.

"Casillas has a reputation for liking innocent girls," he said with distaste as he leaned back in his chair. "And once he found out that you and I had been together, he was no longer interested in helping you out."

She closed her eyes as mortification weighed heavily on her shoulders. Sebastian had discussed their private moment with Raymond? He was just like her womanizing father and his raucous drinking buddies. A wave of disappointment crashed through her. She had expected better of Sebastian. "You're disgusting," she whispered.

"I do what is necessary to win."

He was a worthy opponent. She didn't care if his indiscretion helped her escape Raymond. He was still a dangerous enemy and she needed to remember that. "This isn't over. I will see you in court," she declared as she headed for the door.

"Good luck with that," he called out after her. "You can't afford legal advice and any good lawyer will tell you that you don't have a case."

"Don't underestimate me." She tossed the warning over her shoulder.

"How badly do you want Inez Key?" he asked lazily as she grabbed the door handle.

She dipped her head as she considered the question. How could she explain? Inez Key was more than her home. It was the only thing left of her family yet it was also a constant and unwelcome reminder. It was her sanctuary but it was also her dungeon. She was both caretaker and captive. She was determined to live there until she exorcised her demons. "Probably as much as you did."

His chuckle sent a shiver down her spine. "You shouldn't have told me that."

She turned around and narrowed her eyes. He looked so calm and in control as he lounged in his chair and watched her with barely concealed amusement. "What do you want, Cruz?"

His smile sent a shiver down her spine. "You."

CHAPTER TWO

SEBASTIAN SAW ASHLEY flinch from his answer. He knew she wasn't surprised by his admission. He saw the flare of interest in her eyes and the flush in her cheeks before she tried to shield her reaction. She was trying to hold back her response, but her body was betraying her. She couldn't hide the hectic pulse beating at the base of her neck. Ashley still wanted him, but she wasn't going to admit it.

"You've made it very obvious," Ashley said in a withering tone.

"I'm not ashamed of it." He didn't consider his desire for Ashley a weakness. It was more of a problem, a distraction and a growing obsession. She, on the other hand, was ashamed by the attraction they shared. She acted as if it went against everything she believed in.

"I'm not for sale," she declared.

The corner of his mouth slanted up. "You said the same about Inez Key and look at how that worked out."

Her jaw clenched. "I'm serious, Cruz," she said in a growl.

If she'd been serious, she would have tossed back his

indecent proposal. Used a few choice words and punctuated her indignation with a slap. Instead, she held the door handle in a death grip. She was wavering. Horrified but enthralled. If he played this right he could have Ashley back in his bed for more than a night.

"I'm sure we can work out an arrangement," he said smoothly as the excitement burned inside him. He had ached for her for weeks and the sensation intensified now that he knew the wait was almost over.

"You are no better than Raymond," she said in a hiss.

Sebastian smirked. Her comment just proved how innocent and unworldly she really was. Hadn't she realized by now that he was much, much worse?

"On the contrary, Casillas had set a trap. I'm being extremely honest about what I want." And he wanted Ashley more than anything. It didn't make sense. She wasn't like the other women in his life. She was untamed and inexperienced. Trouble. An inconvenience.

He should cut her loose. After all, he was lying about what he was willing to offer in exchange. He wasn't letting her back on that island. He wasn't going to break a promise just so he could please this spoiled little princess. But he was intrigued to see what her price would be.

"Honest?" she asked, the word exploding from her pink lips. "How can you say that when you introduced yourself under a different name with the intent of seducing the island from me?"

He rose from his seat and approached her. This time she was too angry to be cautious. She didn't catch the scent of danger. Her brown eyes glittered and she thrust out her chin.

Sebastian wondered why she attempted to hide behind the shapeless white dress. Her beauty was too bold, her personality too brash, to be restrained. His palms itched to pull her hair free and watch it tumble past her shoulders. He wanted to smear the pale makeup from her face and reveal the island girl he knew.

"You're the one who isn't being honest," Sebastian said as he stood before her, noticing how her chest rose and fell with agitation. "You knew what Casillas was really after and you didn't disabuse him of that idea because you needed the money."

"I tried the banks but—"

"Casillas makes your skin crawl. Don't you think he knew that? Did you realize that made you even more desirable to him?" Sebastian asked. "You tried to play the game and got in too deep."

Ashley raised an eyebrow. "Did *you* consider that I fell into bed with you because I wanted to get rid of my virginity? That I needed to so I could escape Raymond?"

Sebastian jerked his head back. He had *not* considered that. The possibility ate away at him like acid. He was not going to be used by a pampered princess.

Sebastian gripped her chin with his fingers and held her still. He felt the fight beneath her smooth, silky skin. "Did you?" he asked in a low, angry tone that would send his employees scurrying for safety.

Her eyes gleamed with reckless defiance. "Not so sure anymore, are you?"

He watched her closely as the unfamiliar emotions squeezed his chest. With her natural beauty and independent spirit, Ashley Jones could have had any man. He didn't know why she'd waited for her first sexual experience, but if she needed to get rid of her virginity, she would have picked an uncomplicated man whom she could control.

He stroked the pad of his thumb against her chin as he held his fiery emotions in check. "I think you slept with me because you couldn't help it," he said in a husky voice. She wanted him even though it meant yielding. Surrendering. "Casillas had nothing to do with it. You forgot all about him when you were with me."

She tried to slap his hand away. "Dream on."

He couldn't help but dream about Ashley and the night they had shared. He remembered every touch and kiss. Every gasp and moan. Ashley hadn't been faking it. "You want me so much that it scares you. And that's why you tried to push me away."

"I pushed you away because I didn't want to continue the fling," she argued. "You served your purpose and I was done. I have no interest in playboys."

He dropped his hand. *Served his purpose*? He knew she said that to hide the fact that he would always be a significant part in her love life, but she was going to pay for those words. "I'm not a playboy."

"Ha!" she said bitterly. "You tried to hide it when you were at Inez Key, but I grew up around womanizers. I know what kind of man you are. You would dangle a woman's home as bait, but we both know you will not give it back."

Sebastian bit back a smile. Ashley Jones thought very highly of herself. Did she really believe he would give up his treasure for another taste of what they'd shared? "I never said I'd give back your home."

She went still and frowned. "I don't understand. You asked me—"

"How much you wanted Inez Key," he clarified as he stepped closer, inhaling her citrusy scent. "The ownership of the island is not up for grabs. I keep what is mine and I will not let it slip through my fingers."

Ashley paled and she leaned against the door. "I've taken care of the island for years," she said in a whisper. "I have given it my love, sweat and tears. I've sacrificed everything for it."

"Why?" There was nothing remarkable about the island. It had no natural resources or historical significance. It was in an undesirable location and he had been the only prospective buyer interested in the island.

"Why?" she repeated dully. "It's my home."

Sebastian saw the guarded look in her eyes and knew she wasn't giving the whole answer. He also knew she wouldn't share it with him. She'd learned her lesson and didn't trust him anymore.

There had been moments during that weekend when Ashley had been unguarded and spontaneous. Now she was wary. He ignored the surprising pang of regret. It was time she learned how the real world worked and he had given her a very valuable lesson. "Your attachment to Inez Key doesn't make any sense."

"What about you?" she countered. "Not that many

people would go to such lengths to steal someone's home."

"I didn't steal it," he said with a hint of impatience. "You couldn't pay back the loan so the island is now mine."

"What are your plans for it?" she asked as if it hurt to think of the changes he was going to make. "I can't imagine you want to live there. I'm sure you have many homes. Inez Key is practically roughing it in comparison."

"Don't worry about it," he said as he reached for the door. It was time to force her into making a decision. "Inez Key is now my concern."

Ashley bit her bottom lip as she stared at the open door. The beat of silence stretched until her shoulders slumped. "Cruz."

"The name is Sebastian," he reminded her. She had said his name repeatedly during that one night. She'd said it with wonder and excitement. With longing and satisfaction. And tonight it would be the last thing she said before she fell asleep.

Sebastian. No, she wouldn't call him that. Sebastian had been a mysterious stranger on the island. His intensity and raw masculinity had unleashed a fierce sexual hunger that she hadn't known was in her. She would never be the same again.

This arrogant man was calculating and intimidating. He was breathtaking and she couldn't take her eyes off him. But he was not the fantasy lover she remembered.

Maybe that was the problem. Had she built up that

one magical night in her head? Everything had been so new. Almost foreign. She wouldn't feel overwhelmed from the wild sensations if she had sex with him again. Yet the memory of sharing a bed with Sebastian still made her weak in the knees.

"If you have no intention of giving me back my home," she asked carefully as her heart pounded against her ribs, "what are you offering?"

"You'll be the caretaker and stay in the cottage behind the main house."

She held back the flash of anger. She had been the mistress of the house. She had free rein of the island. Now he was offering the role as caretaker as if it was a gift? "Not good enough."

He placed his finger against her lips. "Careful, *mi vida*," he said softly as his eyes glittered with warning. "I don't have to let you on the island at all. I don't have to let anyone who is living there stay."

She gasped at his thinly veiled threat. "*No*. This has nothing to do with the other families on the island. They've been there for generations."

"You are going to champion the others?" he mocked. "How adorable."

She thought of the five families that lived on the small island. They had been there for her during her darkest moments. Since then, she had provided for them and protected them. She wasn't going to let them down. "Don't interfere with their lives," she said. "This is between you and me."

"Yes, it is," he drawled as he closed the door. Sebastian rested his hand above her head. He was too close. She felt trapped. Cornered.

It was a struggle to remain still and meet his gaze. "What do you want from me?"

"Two weeks in my bed."

Her skin went hot and her mouth dropped open. "I wouldn't stay in your bed for two more minutes, let alone—"

"Make it three," he said coldly.

Her eyes widened. "You bastard." She bit out the words.

"And now it's four," he said with no emotion. "Do you want to make it five weeks?"

A month with Sebastian? The wall she had painstakingly built around herself had shattered after one night with him. What would happen to her after four weeks in his bed?

Now if only she could silence the dark excitement building inside her, threatening to break free. She didn't like this side of her. She was not going to let this sexual hunger govern her thoughts and decisions. She was nothing like her parents.

"Ashley, one month won't be enough for you," he promised.

She pressed her lips together as she struggled to remain silent. She shouldn't have allowed him to rattle her. Her angry words always had consequences.

"It may not even last that long," he said. "I have a short attention span when it comes to women, but you'll beg me to stay."

That was what she was afraid of. She prided herself

on not being a sexual woman, until she met Sebastian Cruz. One look at him and the dormant sensations had sprung violently to life. Her response to his touch had frightened her. She hadn't recognized herself. This man had wielded a power over her like no other.

She was going to break this spell he'd woven. She'd figure out how he lowered her defenses so easily, and kill the craving she had for Sebastian Cruz. And when this month was over, she would never let a man have this kind of hold on her again.

"I want to make sure I understand this," she said shakily. "I will have a home on the island if I share a bed with you for a month?"

"Correct," he said as his eyes held a devilish gleam.

There had to be a catch. Why would he kick her out of the main house only to give her a smaller one on the island? It was convenient for him to have a caretaker who already knew Inez Key, but did he think this arrangement would continue for as long as he wished? "How do I know that you won't fire me?"

"You'll have a contract just like my other employees," he murmured as his attention focused on her mouth.

Her lips stung with awareness. They felt fuller. Softer. She tried not to nervously lick them. "How long do I have before I give you my decision?"

He moved closer, his mouth above hers. She felt his warm breath waft over her skin. "You have to give it to me now."

Alarm jolted through her veins. "Now? That's not

fair!" What was she saying? Sebastian didn't play fair. He played to win.

"Take it or leave it," he said.

She wanted to look away. Find another option. As much as she wanted to stay on Inez Key, she didn't think she was strong enough to fight the desire she had for Sebastian. But she couldn't walk away from this. "I'll take it," she whispered.

Sebastian captured her mouth with his. His kiss was bold, rough and possessive. She wanted to resist. Was determined to give no response. Yet she parted her lips and leaned into him as he deepened the kiss. Their tongues parried as he pulled her closer. She tasted his lust and it thrilled her. She yielded as he conquered her mouth.

Ashley jerked away. *What was wrong with her?* Her heart was racing and she fought the urge to place her fingers on her tingling lips. She couldn't look at Sebastian. She was confused. Aroused. Her emotions had been ambushed.

How could she have responded so eagerly? For him? Sebastian Cruz represented everything she despised in a man. "I need to leave," she said as she clumsily reached for the door handle. "I have a few things I need to deal with back home."

"You're not going home." Sebastian wrapped his hand around her wrist and pulled her hand away from the door. "You will return to Inez Key on my terms."

She stared at him as his calmly delivered words filtered into her jumbled mind. He wasn't allowing her to go home? How dare he? But then, it wasn't her home anymore. Technically, it was his. "I said I would share a bed with you. There was nothing—"

"You are now my mistress," he said as he raised her hand and pressed his lips against the skittering pulse on her wrist. "You live where I live. Sleep where I sleep."

Mistress? Her knees threatened to give out. She hated that word. Her dad had kept many mistresses. Vulgar women who didn't care who they hurt as long as they got the attention they felt they deserved. "I didn't agree to that."

"I didn't say that I would share my nights with you," he reminded her. "I am sharing a bed. That could happen at any time of day. Or all day."

All day. The wicked excitement pulled low in her belly. No, this was bad. This was really bad. What had she gotten herself into?

"Backing out already?" he said in a purr.

This was her chance. She could extract herself from this agreement and run back to her safe little world. But that world no longer existed. He owned it. Now she had to fight for a little piece of it. Ashley swallowed roughly. "No."

"Good." Sebastian's satisfaction vibrated in his deep voice as he pulled the door open and led her out of his office.

"Where are we going?" she asked, stumbling in her heels as she tried to keep up with him.

"To get you out of that dress."

She went rigid. He wanted to seal the deal *now?* She wasn't ready. Her mind froze yet her nipples tightened in anticipation as her legs went limp.

"I'm calling a stylist," Sebastian announced. "The dress you're wearing hides your body and ages you about two decades."

She didn't care. She didn't like dressing up or bringing attention to her body. Her clothes were meant to fade into the background. "Why do I need another dress?"

"I have an event I must attend and you are coming with me," he said as they reached his private elevator.

An event? No doubt it was glamorous and luxurious. There would be the Miami elite attending. Many of them would be the friends and former lovers of her parents. It was going to be a nightmare. "I don't want to go."

"You don't know much about being a mistress, do you?" he asked as he wrapped his arm around her waist and dragged her against him. "You really don't have a say in the matter."

Ashley was very aware of his hand spanning the small of her back. She felt delicate, almost fragile, next to him. She didn't like it. "Are you aware that there's a difference between mistress and sex slave?"

"Try not to put ideas into my head," he murmured.

The last thing she wanted was to be seen in public on the arm of the most unapologetic playboy. After years of shielding herself from the tabloids that had been fascinated with her parents' escapades, she didn't want the world to see how far she had fallen.

No one would be surprised, though. She was, after all, the daughter of Linda Valdez and Donald Jones. "I thought men hid their mistresses," she complained under her breath, "not showed them off."

"You have a lot to learn, Ashley," he said as his hold tightened on her waist. "I'm looking forward to teaching you everything."

CHAPTER THREE

How HAD SHE got to this point? Ashley stared at her reflection in the full-length mirror. Sebastian had brought in a stylist and hairdresser to his penthouse apartment at the top of his office building and they had spent the past few hours getting her ready for the night. Most women would have found it fun and relaxing. She thought it had been pure torture.

Her eyes were wide and her hands were clenched at her sides. The sumptuous walk-in closet faded in the background as she focused on her wild mane of hair. Her gaze traveled from her red lips to her stiletto heels. There was something familiar about the look.

Was this how all of Sebastian's women dressed? She couldn't live up to this sexual promise. This outfit, this look, was for a woman whose only goal was to please a man. Who placed her worth on whom she could attract and how long she could keep the man interested. She had seen plenty of women like that while she was growing up.

Ashley frowned and studied the orange dress a little closer. Why would Sebastian want a woman who didn't make any demands? He didn't seem to be the type who would surround himself with vapid women who didn't challenge his intellect. But then, she didn't know much about his love life.

Love? She snorted at the word. Sex, she mentally corrected herself. His sex life. If she asked him, would he remember all his lovers or were his women indistinguishable, one from the other?

The possibility pricked sharply at her. She didn't want to be grouped with those women. Nameless and forgettable. She couldn't go out looking like this. Like one of his mistresses. The dress wasn't as revealing as she'd feared, but the daring attitude carried more than a promise of sex. It suggested her status and her price.

She abruptly turned her head and a memory collided with the movement she saw in the mirror. She froze. *No, no, no!* Slowly looking back, Ashley stared at her reflection with a mix of panic and horror. Big hair. Little dress. Bold color.

For a moment, she resembled her mother.

Linda Valdez had always worn bright and daring colors. She had wanted Donald Jones to notice her whether she was watching his tennis match from the players' box or whether she was in a room filled with nubile women. When that didn't work, Linda's dresses started to get shorter and more revealing. She had been afraid to change her hairstyle in case it displeased Donald.

Everything her mother had done was to keep Donald's interest. If his eyes strayed on to another woman, Linda would become desperate for his attention. Ashley knew her father never cared about her mother's interests or opinions; his only concern was that Linda was beautiful, sexually available to him, and that everyone knew it. He would dress Linda in cheap and tasteless clothes and publicly discuss their relationship in the crudest language.

Ashley squeezed her eyes shut as she remembered one dress her mother had refused to wear. The bright red dress had been unforgiving. The corset bodice had painfully thrust Linda's breasts out while the tight skirt had puckered and stretched around her bottom.

Her mother had been extraordinarily beautiful, but that unflattering outfit had exaggerated her curves and made her appear almost cartoonish. Yet what Ashley remembered most was, despite the epic argument about the dress, her mother had reluctantly worn it. That dress represented the inequality in her parents' relationship. Ashley remembered clearly how Linda had hunched her shoulders and bent her head in shame when she wore that dress, defeated and humiliated.

Ashley's nails bit into her palms and she choked back the panic. She fought the urge to kick off the delicate heels and rip off the dress. She wanted to get them off before they tainted her.

It was too late. The clothes weren't the problem. Ashley flattened her hand on the mirror and bent her head as she exhaled shakily. For years she had been determined not to follow in her mother's footsteps. She didn't dress up for a man or try to gain his attention. She didn't barter with her looks. And yet, here she was, a rich man's plaything.

The only difference was that her mother had worked

hard to gain Donald Jones's attention. It had taken strategy to become his mistress. She had tried to bump up her status to become a trophy wife with an "unplanned" pregnancy. Unfortunately, Linda Valdez had not been Donald's favorite trophy.

"You are nothing like Mom," Ashley whispered to herself. She made sure of it. Once she thought her mother had been as perfect as a fairy-tale princess and she wanted to be like her. But as Linda got older, and Donald refused to marry her or give her his name, she became more insecure. She felt her beauty fading and knew she was losing the battle with her younger competitors.

Linda Valdez had been beautiful but fragile. Jealous and tempestuous. Ashley had seen the dark side of love and passion even before her mother had killed Donald before turning the gun on herself.

Ashley had been eighteen when that happened. Before that fateful moment she had been wary of men and kept her distance. As she struggled with the aftermath and scandal of the murder-suicide, she knew she would never allow love or sex to influence her life. Ashley had suppressed her passionate nature and hid on Inez Key. She didn't mind being celibate. She had believed sex wasn't worth the tears and heartache.

There were times when the isolation was almost too much to bear. But it was better than what she had witnessed in her parents' relationship. She was ready to spend her life that way until Sebastian showed up on her island.

She had relaxed her guard under his charm and attention. One night with him and her quiet, contained life had spun wildly out of control. Even now, a month later, she found it difficult to hold back. She was too aware of him. Too needy for his touch.

Sebastian had proven her deepest fear. Ashley knew that she was very much her mother's daughter. She was stronger and more disciplined, but she had been wild in Sebastian's arms. The desire had been primal. Almost uncontrollable. She hadn't been the same since. She didn't want to feel the heights of passion because she knew the crash and burn was inevitable. If she wasn't careful, she would succumb to the same torment as her mother.

Sebastian glanced at his watch and strode to the door leading to the walk-in closet. He was not used to waiting for a woman. They followed his schedule and didn't cause any inconvenience. Ashley needed to learn that she was no different. He would not give her any special treatment. "Ashley, I'm not a patient man. It's time to leave."

As much as he would like to stay in and reacquaint himself with Ashley's curves, this was one party he couldn't miss. Wouldn't. The opening of his newest club would bring in hundreds of thousands for charity. His old neighborhood needed that money. And yet, even now, he was tempted to strip off his gray suit, knock down the door and reclaim Ashley. He went hard as he imagined sinking into her welcoming body.

"Ashley?" he snapped.

"Have fun without me," she said through the door.

Sebastian closed his eyes and inhaled sharply. He should have known that she would pout and sulk. Heiresses. It didn't matter if they lived in stilettos or sandals. Each of them knew how to throw a tantrum.

"You're coming with me," he said in a low voice. "That's the agreement."

"Actually, I didn't agree to it," she said, her voice loud and clear. "I said I'd share your bed. I didn't say anything about dressing up like a whore and being put on display to stroke your ego."

Whore? Sebastian shook his head. The dress and shoes were bought at one of the most exclusive boutiques in South Beach. He had paid the hairstylist and makeup artist an exorbitant fee to give Ashley a natural look.

Even if Ashley rolled out of bed and only wore a wrinkled sheet, she couldn't look like a whore. There was something in the way she carried herself. She acted like a queen. Like she was too good for the rest of the world. Too good for him.

"Fine," Sebastian said as he walked away from the door. He could find another woman in a matter of minutes. Someone who was so grateful to be on his arm that she wouldn't challenge him every step of the way. "You don't want Inez Key that much. Understandable. It really isn't much of an island."

"Wait," she called out.

Sebastian hesitated. He didn't wait for anyone. That was one benefit he discovered after making his first million. The powerful people who used to ignore and instantly dismiss him would now wait endlessly for a minute of his time. Why should he treat Ashley any differently?

And yet he was compelled to turn around. Because he wanted Ashley. No other woman would do. She had already invaded his dreams and captured his imagination. When Ashley wrenched the door open and stood defiantly in the threshold, his breath caught in his throat.

Her long brown hair fell past her shoulders in thick waves. He bunched his hands as he remembered how soft and heavy it felt. His gaze drifted down to her face. Only the scowl marred her exquisite beauty.

He couldn't stop staring. The thin leather dress was perfect for Ashley. The casual design made him think of the oversize T-shirts she favored, yet the burnt-orange color reminded him of the sunset they'd shared on Inez Key.

"Perfect," he said gruffly.

She skimmed her hands uncertainly against the metallic embellishments that gave the simple dress an edge. "Did you choose this?"

Sebastian shook his head. "I told the stylist what I expected." He'd wanted something that had symbolized the weekend they'd shared in Inez Key. He didn't know that the dress would cling to her curves and accentuate her sun-kissed skin. His gaze gravitated to her long, toned legs. He remembered how they felt wrapped tightly around his waist. Sebastian swallowed roughly as his mouth felt dry.

"It's too short." She tugged at the hem that barely skimmed the top of her thighs. "Too revealing. Too—"

"Sexy as hell," he said in a growl.

Ashley's breath lodged painfully in her lungs as she watched Sebastian advance. She took a step back and bumped against the door frame. The man moved quietly, like a jungle cat ready to pounce, and she stood before him like helpless prey. Her heart was already beating hard when she saw him. Now it wanted to explode out of her chest.

Ashley wasn't sure how she was going to get out of this situation. She wasn't sure if she *wanted* to. She liked how he looked at her. Liked this tension that coiled around them, excluding everything else. She felt beautiful, powerful and vibrantly alive. Only Sebastian made her feel this way.

But how many other women had felt like this with Sebastian? Her pulse skipped hard as the question bloomed in her mind. Just as he was about to reach her, Ashley held up her hand to stop him. She hoped he didn't see how her fingers trembled. "Not so fast."

"Don't worry, *mi vida*," he said, his voice husky and seductive. "It will be slow and steady."

"That's not what I meant." She felt the heat flood her face as she imagined Sebastian exploring her body, taking his time while she begged for completion. Begged for more. "First, some ground rules."

He raised an eyebrow. "You can't be serious."

Were mistresses not allowed to negotiate? She found that hard to believe. What they had was a business deal. "Do not tell anyone about this arrangement," Ashley demanded as she crossed her arms, forming a barrier. She knew how men bragged. She remembered hearing her father discuss his conquests to any man who'd listen. Each story got bolder and raunchier as the men tried to one-up each other. "This is a private matter."

Sebastian watched her carefully. She couldn't tell if he was offended by her request or if he didn't know why it was worth mentioning. "I don't discuss my private life," he confided in a low voice. "And I won't let anyone talk about you."

Ashley blinked. She wasn't expecting that answer or the sincerity in his dark eyes. Sebastian Cruz was a good liar. He knew what she wanted to hear. If she didn't know that he would say or do anything to get his way, she'd almost believe him.

"Anything else?" he drawled as he moved closer, towering over her.

Ashley felt the pulse fluttering at the base of her throat. His scent, his heat, excited her. But she had one demand that wasn't negotiable. If he denied her this, she would walk out immediately. "You will have to use protection."

He reached out and brushed his knuckle along the line of her jaw. She shivered with anticipation at the gentle touch. "I always do."

"Always?" she taunted. Womanizers didn't think much about the future. They focused on instant gratification. It was the women who had to protect themselves and deal with the consequences alone.

"Always," he repeated as his fingertips grazed her throat and shoulder. "I take care of my lovers."

Sure. That had to be the real reason. It had nothing

to do with giving up control. "And you wouldn't want a gold digger to get pregnant and live off your money."

Sebastian's eyes flashed with agreement. "Any more rules?"

Ashley nervously licked her lips with the tip of her tongue. She wanted to create a list of rules, but her mind was blank. "No..."

"Good." Sebastian wrapped his fingers around her wrists. His hold was firm and commanding. She gasped when he held her hands high above her head. He leaned into her and Ashley hated how her body yielded to him. Her soft breasts were thrust against his hard chest and her pelvis cradled his erection. Sebastian surrounded her.

His powerful thigh wedged between her shaky legs. "Now, for my ground rules."

Ashley swallowed hard. She should have expected he would have rules of his own. She was ready to refuse them all, but she was secretly intrigued. She wanted to know what he demanded from a woman.

"First," he said as he pressed his mouth against her cheekbone, "you are available to me twenty-four hours a day."

"You don't ask for much, do you?" she asked sarcastically as the excitement clawed up her chest.

"And you have no claim on me," Sebastian said as he kissed his way down the curve of her throat. She couldn't refrain from arching her neck and encouraging more. "When I want you, I will call for you."

Now, *that* she had expected from Sebastian. He would decide when and where. Any affair would meet his schedule and the woman would have to learn how to adapt.

"Maybe you don't understand," Ashley said, closing her eyes as his hot breath warmed her skin. "I'm not the kind of woman who sits around and waits."

"You will be with me." His mouth hovered against her wildly beating pulse point at the base of her throat. He circled it with the tip of his tongue, silently showing that he knew how he made her feel. "It will be worth the wait."

She took in a ragged gulp of air. "You talk big—"

He cupped her cheeks with his large hands and kissed her. She was ready to counterattack, but he disarmed her immediately. His lips were demanding as he drew her tongue inside his mouth. She was out of control, mindlessly following his lead as the desire bled inside her.

When he withdrew, Ashley saw the stain of lipstick on his firm mouth and the way his eyes glittered knowingly. "I know how much you want this. Want *me*."

She was embarrassed at her response. Humiliated that he stopped the kiss. She felt scorched. Boneless. Ashley remembered feeling like this. Sebastian knew exactly how to touch her. She wanted more and yet she wanted it to stop. She needed to take control but at the same time she wanted to throw caution to the wind and see where she landed.

"Anything else?" she asked hoarsely.

His hand grazed her breast and he drew lazy circles around her hard nipple with his fingertip. "I expect total obedience from my women."

She flinched. She wasn't sure which part of his rule bothered her. The fact that she was lumped into a group known as "his women"? Or the obedience part? She wasn't going to let this man—or any man—master her. She wasn't a plaything. "Following the rules has never been my strength," she said.

"You'll learn. All you need is the right motivation." Sebastian smiled as he trailed his fingertips down her rib cage. His touch was as light as a feather and yet her skin tingled with awareness.

"I can't promise you obedience," she said between pants. "In fact, I won't."

Her words made him smile. "I can make you promise anything."

She wanted to give a bitter laugh. Slap his hand away. Tell him he was only fooling himself. But deep down she knew Sebastian could have that power, and she didn't want to test it. "You are very sure of yourself."

He didn't reply. Instead, he splayed his hand between her thighs. Sebastian's eyes held an unholy gleam when he realized she wore nothing underneath her dress. He murmured his approval in Spanish as he began to stroke the folds of her sex.

Ashley immediately clamped her legs together but it was too late. Sebastian wasn't going to let that deter him. He gave a husky laugh of triumph as she responded. She looked away as the liquid heat flooded her body.

"Look at me," he said roughly.

Ashley shook her head. She couldn't look in his eyes and show him how she felt. How he made her feel. From his expert touch, it was obvious that he already knew. The humiliation burned and yet she bucked against his hand.

She wouldn't look at him. And yet she couldn't tell him to stop. She didn't want to push him away. She felt the white heat whipping through her, catching fire. Her fear was that he would stop unless she followed his command.

Sebastian growled. "Look at me," he repeated.

She squeezed her eyes shut and shook her head again. A guttural moan escaped from deep in her chest as Sebastian dipped his finger into her clenching core. Ashley felt his hot gaze. She knew he saw everything. He knew what she wanted. What if he held back? Oh, God…what if he didn't stop until she revealed her deepest need and darkest fantasy?

"Ashley." His voice was raw and urgent.

She was compelled to open her eyes. Ashley met his intense gaze just as the climax rippled through her. Her mouth sagged open and her muscles locked as she chased the pleasure. Sebastian saw everything and she couldn't hide. How was he going to use this to his advantage?

He slowly, almost reluctantly, withdrew from her. Ashley ached from the loss and she sagged against the wall. Her body trembled. She wanted to hold on to him, but she wouldn't dare.

"Total obedience," he reminded her quietly.

His words were like a slap. Was this a display of his dominance? Did he want to prove that he could make her do whatever he wished?

Ashley pushed away from him and smoothed her dress with clumsy hands. She would not submit to his will. "No, Cruz," she said as she fought to stand straight on wobbly legs. "That will never happen."

"Haven't you learned by now, Ashley?" he asked as the challenge glinted in his eyes. "I always get what I want."

CHAPTER FOUR

As ASHLEY STOOD in the VIP section of Sebastian's dance club, she couldn't help but feel as if she had fallen into the looking glass. The flashing lights were hypnotic and the dancers moved to the music as if they were in a trance. She had never seen a place like this before. It was fantastical. Otherworldly and a little frightening.

And this was just part of Sebastian's kingdom. The moment they entered, she had felt the ripple of interest and awe. At first she had been uncomfortable being in the spotlight, but as Sebastian spoke to members of the Miami elite, she realized she was invisible to the guests. They lobbied for Sebastian's attention and saw no need to speak to her. She was arm candy. An expensive accessory.

She should feel grateful that no one noticed or cared about her. She recognized a few of her parents' friends, but they didn't seem to remember her. She felt small and powerless in the cavernous club. More than once, Ashley wondered how much of the club reflected Sebastian's personality. It was darkly sensual and seductive. The music pulsated from the floor and she tried to ignore the carnal rhythm, but her heartbeat matched the tempo.

The wild laughter punctuating the air made her flinch. She didn't want to be here, around these people who had enjoyed her parents' downfall. Ashley wished she was back on Inez Key. It was quiet and relaxing. Calm and predictable. That was where she belonged. It had been *her* kingdom.

But there had been a time when she'd needed to get away from her island. Sebastian must have known that. She remembered the unexpected fun she'd had with Sebastian on that weekend when he let her take his boat out for a spin.

The offer had been too tantalizing to resist. She loved being out on the water and had wanted to try his speedboat. At the time, she had thought her acceptance had nothing to do with the promise of having Sebastian's undivided attention.

Ashley had known the boat would slice through the choppy waves and reach incredible speed. She had wanted to go on a fast-and-hard ride, determined to forget Inez Key and her financial problems for a few hours.

She remembered Sebastian's warm smile as he had teased her, suggesting she was trying to tip him out of the boat. Perhaps she had been trying to test his courage. She had to find out if his restraint had just been a guise. Ashley had wanted to know how long it would take before he grabbed the wheel.

He never did. Sebastian had been lazily sprawled on the chair next to her, arms outstretched, his dark glasses perched on his bold nose. Sexual heat had bubbled underneath their banter, but she had enjoyed his companionship.

Sebastian had been relaxed and unconcerned while she made hairpin turns and the boat flew over the waves, but he had been alert. He had noticed every move she made, offering the occasional direction only when she hesitated.

Ashley had to wonder if any of that rapport had been real or part of the seduction. Had he done that to lower her guard or had he enjoyed those moments, too? Looking around this nightclub, she sensed the simple joy of a sunny afternoon would have been lost on him.

She glanced up, her heart lurching to a stop as she watched gorgeous couples dance with unbridled enthusiasm on the mezzanine. Their movements were bold and suggestive. Her skin flushed and she shifted uncomfortably. She was already painfully aware of Sebastian and primed for his touch. She didn't need anything else to encourage her imagination.

Her grip tightened on her small clutch purse and she fought the urge to retreat. The club was mysterious and spellbinding. Dangerous. Much like it's owner. If she lowered her guard, the music would pull her in. The atmosphere would seduce her into releasing her inhibitions. That could ruin her. Take her to a point of no return.

Ashley studied the DJ booth and the small VIP areas that circled the dance floor. She recognized a few movie stars and professional athletes lounging on the big white couches with other celebrities and models. All of the party girls were glamorous creatures with wild hair and generous curves.

"And how is your mother doing?"

Ashley turned sharply as she caught the question. A trio of beautiful women were standing in front of Sebastian. She didn't know which one asked the question. They all looked similar with their smooth hair, flawless makeup and colorful dresses that wrapped around them like skimpy bath towels.

"She's recuperating well," Sebastian replied before he smoothly changed the subject. Within moments he had the group of women giggling and fawning all over him.

Ashley wondered if she was the only one who noticed the way his features softened at the mention of his mother. Or the flash of worry in his eyes before he banked it. She wished she hadn't seen it. She didn't want to know anything about him. The less she knew about his private life, the better.

What they shared was a business agreement and she needed to keep an emotional distance. She was having a short-term sexual relationship with Sebastian and she wasn't required to love, respect or even *like* the man.

So what if he had been the most fascinating and exciting man when they first met? Sebastian had been playing a role. Or had he? She thought she had seen glimpses of the real Sebastian during the quieter moments on Inez Key. It was as if the island life had pulled away the harsh mask and revealed his romantic nature.

That was not his true character, she reminded herself fiercely as disappointment rested heavily in her chest.

She wasn't going to be like her mother, who clung to her benefactor's rare thoughtful gestures and created a fairy-tale love story out of it. There was nothing Sebastian could do to make her think he was anything other than a cold-hearted and ruthless womanizer.

"Sebastian!"

Ashley lifted her head when she heard a booming male voice over the music. She saw a large, muscular man approach Sebastian with his arms outstretched. The stranger was about the same age as Sebastian but was built like a giant. The curvy blonde woman at his side looked tiny in comparison.

"Omar," Sebastian greeted. Ashley was startled by Sebastian's wide smile and the way his face lit up before he embraced his friend.

She was more surprised that Sebastian *had* friends. Sebastian could be charming and a scintillating conversationalist, but for some reason, she assumed he was a loner. An outsider.

"And who is this?" Omar asked, gesturing at Ashley while Sebastian gave the other woman a kiss on the cheek.

Ashley felt a twinge of fear. Omar was obviously a good friend. Would Sebastian lie to spare her embarrassment? Why would he do that? Yes, he'd made her a promise, but his friend was going to be more important than a temporary mistress.

She didn't trust Sebastian. She had to get in front of this before he showed just how little power she had in this arrangement. Ashley thrust out her hand to Omar. "I'm Ashley."

Sebastian wrapped a proprietary arm around her waist as his friend shook her hand. "Omar and I grew up in the same neighborhood before he became a football star."

Ashley nodded as she tried to fit this new information in with what she knew about Sebastian. She didn't expect him to value friendships from his old world. She had seen a few self-made men who had discarded old friends while in pursuit of making strategic alliances. Sebastian wasn't as ruthless or driven as she thought.

"And this is my wife, Crystal," Omar introduced the blonde.

"It's a pleasure to meet you," Ashley said as she greeted Omar's wife. The woman was beautiful, but Ashley recognized the subtle signs of multiple cosmetic surgeries. Most of the women she knew while growing up had the same unlined forehead, puffy lips and enhanced breasts.

"I like your dress," Crystal said as the two men started speaking to each other in Spanish.

"Thank you," Ashley said as she pulled at the short hem. She was still uncomfortable in it, but it wasn't as revealing as Crystal's. Most of the women in the club wore dresses that were staying on their bodies with little more than double-sided tape and a prayer.

Crystal gave a cursory glance over her outfit as if she was adding up the price. "Who are you wearing?"

Who? Oh, right. She remembered this part of the social world that she used to belong to. It was all about getting the designer bag or dress that no one else had.

She had once been like that until her world came crashing down. "I forgot to ask about the designer."

Crystal shook her head as if she couldn't believe Ashley would forget such an important detail. "So how did you two meet?"

Ashley glanced at Sebastian, but he was involved in an animated conversation with his friend. She hadn't come up with a cover story but she knew she had to be very careful. It was best to keep it as close to the truth as possible. "I met him a month ago. We immediately hit it off."

"I'm surprised," Crystal said as she studied Ashley, as if she was cataloging all of her flaws and shortcomings. "You're not really his type."

"What is his type?" Ashley asked reluctantly, not entirely sure if she wanted the answer.

Crystal gave a laugh of disbelief. "You don't know?"

She shrugged. "I didn't know who Sebastian truly was until it was too late."

"How is that possible? He's in the news all the time. From the financial page to the gossip column. Have you been living under a rock?"

"More like a deserted island."

Crystal frowned as if she wasn't sure Ashley's comments was a joke or the truth. "Well, I would say Sebastian's women are more…"

"Blonde?" Ashley supplied wearily. "Curvaceous? Vacuous?"

"Accomplished," Crystal corrected her.

Ashley's muscles stiffened. That hurt. She wasn't proud of where she was in her life. She had fallen in

status and wealth. Her world had become smaller and
she was no match for Sebastian. But she had achieved
more than she thought was possible. She had taken care
of the families on Inez Key. She maintained her island
home with nothing more than ingenuity and hard work.
Her most important accomplishment had been becoming a woman who was nothing like her mother.

Ashley was proud that she hadn't broken under the
heavy burden placed on her five years ago, but she
wasn't going to share that. Not with Crystal or anyone
at the nightclub. They would belittle it. Dismiss it. Sneer
at her. She remembered this world. All the guests cared
about was being noticed. They would never understand
that her greatest achievement was creating a peaceful
life hidden from the spotlight.

"Accomplished? You mean famous," Ashley corrected.

Crystal shrugged. "They are the best in their fields
or famous for their philanthropy and humanitarian efforts. He's dated CEOs and pro athletes. Politicians and
princesses."

"I guess he doesn't feel threatened by a woman's
achievements," she said with a fixed smile. If this was
true, what was he doing with her? She had struggled
in school and dropped out of college in her first semester. She had no skills or special talents. No ambi-
tions other than to build the strong and happy family
life she'd never had.

"Don't get me wrong," Crystal continued, as if her
words hadn't pierced Ashley's thin guard, "he's had
his share of supermodels and movie stars. He's just

not interested in a woman whose goal is to be a wife or a girlfriend."

What about a mistress? Not that she strived for that job. She had been blackmailed into bed because she had no power or influential friends. Ashley bit the tip of her tongue in case she blurted out her thoughts.

Crystal tilted her head. "I feel like I've seen you before."

Ashley stiffened. She remembered comments like that. It only took a few moments before they connected her with one of her father's scandals. "I haven't been in Miami for years."

"Have you been in the news lately? I have to admit, I'm a bit of a news junkie," Crystal said as she pressed her bejeweled hand over her impressive cleavage. "TV, newspapers, blogs, tabloids. I get my news anywhere and everywhere."

"No, I haven't done anything newsworthy."

"Crystal, they are playing our song," Omar said as he wrapped his large hand over his wife's wrist. "It's time to hit the dance floor."

Sebastian watched Ashley as her frown deepened. She hadn't spoken much. She had stood at his side, but he knew she wasn't paying attention to her surroundings.

Was she was thinking about tonight? How she would lose control in his arms? She had no idea that he also couldn't stop thinking about the magical night that lay ahead. Or that he would make sure she lost control before he did.

He didn't know how much longer his restraint would

last. Having her close to him, touching him, was a test. He was careful not to stroke her skin or allow his hand to linger on the curve of her hip. Once he started, he wouldn't stop.

He tightened his hold on her waist. "Smile, Ashley."

Ashley gave a start and then glared at him. "I am smiling."

"No, you're not." He dipped his head and pressed his mouth against her ear. She shivered with awareness and his body clenched in response. "But I know one way I can put a smile on your face."

She yanked her head back and bared her teeth. "I'm smiling, I'm smiling. See?"

"Can you look less bloodthirsty and more adoring?"

"Why? The only people who looked at me were Omar and Crystal." She tugged at her short hem again. "Don't get me wrong, Cruz. I'm grateful that I'm un-recognizable. I can only assume I look like all your other mistresses."

He'd never had a mistress, but she didn't need to know that. He didn't want her to get any ideas that she was different or special. He'd had many lovers, but he'd never had to pay for the exclusive rights of a woman.

"And how much longer do we have to stay here?" she asked.

"Eager for bed, *mi vida*?" He certainly was. He hadn't felt this desperate since he was a teenager. It was difficult to circulate among the crowd when he wanted to drag Ashley to his bedroom.

She clenched her jaw. "No, I'm tired of acting like I know what's going on. Your guests talk about people

I don't know and places I haven't been. I wasn't aware that you were raising money for a charity until you talked that socialite into giving double. Where is the money going?"

"To my old neighborhood," he said tersely. He briefly closed his eyes as he tried to banish the memory of graffiti-stained walls and the stench of rotted garbage.

She sighed. "Can you be a little more specific?"

"You wouldn't recognize the address. It's the ghetto," he said with a hint of defiance and anger. He should have had the idyllic childhood that Ashley had enjoyed. While her life had been luxurious and carefree, his days had been difficult and unsafe. He'd had to fend for himself and his family and there were many early days when he had failed.

He'd left the ghetto years ago, but he had honed his survival instincts in his old neighborhood. Stay alert, know how to fight and shut down any potential threat before it gained power. Those rules helped him in the streets and in building his empire.

Her eyelashes flickered. "You're right. I don't know where that is, but only because I don't get out much. And the money is for...?"

"The medical clinic," he said slowly as he watched her expression. She showed no pity or fear. No disdain about his background. Just polite interest. Considering her sheltered and privileged life, Sebastian wondered if she understood living in the ghetto was like a prison term.

He grabbed her hand, ignoring how it fit perfectly in his, and led her out of the VIP section. "Let's dance."

He couldn't wait anymore. He needed to feel her curves flush against his body.

Ashley froze and dug her heels in. "I don't dance."

Sebastian stopped and turned around. "You don't dance. You don't drink. You don't party." He didn't believe any of it. He knew many heiresses and socialites. They lived to be seen at the right places with the right people. "What do you do?"

Ashley shrugged and looked away. "Nothing that would interest you."

It shouldn't interest him. He didn't care what women did when they weren't with him. Sebastian didn't want to know about their jobs, hobbies or passions. Yet he was intensely curious about Ashley. "You don't date."

She looked at him cautiously from the corner of her eye. "I never said that."

She didn't have to. "I was your first," he reminded her. And for some reason that was important to him. Was it because she was his first virgin? He didn't like the possessive streak that heated his blood and made him want to keep her close.

"I've been busy," she declared as she tried to slip from his grasp.

"Busy doing what?" he asked as he pulled her closer. How did she fill her day? "You live in a tropical paradise. You don't have a job or obligations. Most people would kill for that kind of life."

"Is that what you think?" She abruptly stopped and pressed her lips together. "Okay, sure. My life is perfect. And that's why I will go to great lengths to keep it."

Sebastian narrowed his eyes as he watched Ashley's guarded expression. What was she hiding? He was about to go in for the kill when he felt a feminine hand on his sleeve.

"Sebastian?"

He recognized the cultured voice before he turned around and saw the cool blonde standing next to him. He dropped his hold on Ashley as he greeted his former flame with a kiss on the cheek. "Hello, Melanie," he said.

"And who is this?" she asked with false brightness.

Sebastian swallowed back a sigh. This always seemed to happen when an ex-lover met the current one. He found the territorial attitude tiresome. "Melanie, this is Ashley Jones. Ashley, this is Dr. Melanie Guerra. She works at the medical clinic."

"And I'm also your predecessor," Melanie said bitterly as she shook Ashley's hand. "I believe you stole him from me."

"Would you like him back?" Ashley asked hopefully.

Melanie was momentarily surprised before she gave a shrill of laughter. Sebastian wrapped his hand around Ashley's arm and shot her a warning look. He wasn't sure what Ashley was going to do next. It was a rare feeling.

"No, thanks," Melanie said as she gave Ashley a thorough look. "Our fling was very brief and he dumped me after he came back from some island off the Florida coast. I got a bouquet of flowers, a bracelet from Tiffany and no explanation. Now I understand why."

Ashley went rigid under Sebastian's grasp. To his surprise, Ashley didn't respond to Melanie's statement.

Her expression was blank, but he sensed her slow burn of anger.

"She's not really an upgrade, is she, Sebastian?" Melanie said. She smiled, knowing she had dropped a bomb, and strolled away with her head held high.

"I apologize for her, Ashley," he said roughly. "Melanie isn't known for her tact or manners."

"I'm sure that wasn't what drew you to her in the first place," Ashley replied, her eyes flashing with anger. "You were dating her when you slept with me. Are you with someone now?"

"I'm with you." He didn't want anyone else. No woman compared to her and he didn't know why.

"Is there anyone else?" she asked insistently as she tugged away from his grasp.

"What if there was?" he asked. She had no claim, no power over him, and he would remind her of that every moment of this agreement. "What would you do about it? What *could* you do about it?"

She thrust her chin out with pride. "I'd leave."

He scoffed at her declaration. "No, you wouldn't." She wouldn't walk away from him. She'd entered this agreement because she wanted to explore the pleasure they shared.

"Inez Key means everything to me, but—"

"It has nothing to do with the island," he said. He wasn't going to let her hide behind that reason. "You got a taste of what it's like between us and you crave it."

She crossed her arms and glared at him. "No, I don't."

"It's okay, *mi vida*," he said in a confidential tone. "I crave it, too."

"Of course you do. You're insatiable," she argued. "It doesn't matter who you are sleeping with as long as you have a woman in your bed. You're like all men who are ruled by lust and—"

"I'm not an animal," he replied as the anger roughed his voice. "I don't sleep with every woman who flirts with me. I can control my baser instincts. You, I'm not so sure about."

She gasped and took a step back. He saw the surprise and guilt flicker in her dark brown eyes. "What are you talking about?" she asked, her eyes wide.

"You can't wait to go to bed with me," he said with a satisfied smile as the desire swirled inside him. When they finally got to be alone, he knew she was going to go wild. The anticipation kicked harder in his veins.

"I can't wait to get this agreement over with, if that's what you're talking about," she said. "And you didn't answer my question. Are you with another woman right now?"

Ashley was tenacious. "You have no right to ask me that question."

She tossed back her hair and raised an eyebrow. "Because I'm your mistress?"

"Exactly." He splayed his arms out with exasperation. "You really don't have an understanding on how this arrangement works."

"And you don't seem to understand how I function," she retorted. "If you're in a relationship with someone,

I'm going to leave. Play any mind games with me and you will regret it."

He knew she was bluffing, but her voice held a hardened edge. As if she was talking from a past experience. "You'll lose the island."

Ashley leaned forward. "And you won't get another night with me," she said with false sweetness. "Those cravings you have will just get stronger and there will be nothing you can do about it."

Their gazes clashed and held. It was time to teach Ashley a lesson. She suspected just how much he wanted her and was testing her power over him. He wasn't going to let her get away with it.

He heard a feminine squeal of delight next to him. "Sebastian!"

Sebastian reluctantly turned as a woman wrapped her arms around his shoulders and clung to him. He barely recognized the model who had flirted with him a few weeks ago and he couldn't remember her name. She was an exotic creature, but she didn't capture his imagination like Ashley.

"It's been forever since I've seen you," the model declared before she brazenly kissed him on the mouth.

Knowing that Ashley was watching, Sebastian didn't pull away. He wasn't going to allow Ashley to make any demands on him.

Ashley hunched her shoulders as the bile-green jealousy rolled through her. The conflicting emotions were ripping her in shreds. She wanted to pull the other woman away and yet she felt the need to hurt Sebastian the way he was hurting her.

She looked away, unable to see Sebastian in the arms of another woman. She hated this feeling. The ferocity scared her. She didn't know if she could contain it. Ashley jerkily turned away. She refused to live this way for even a moment. She wouldn't tolerate this, even if it meant losing her family home forever.

Ashley pushed her way through the dance floor. She was dragged in and then thrust from side to side as she bumped against dancers. She gritted her teeth and placed a shaky hand on her churning stomach. She had to get out of here.

Forcing herself not to look back, Ashley wasn't even going to think about where she could go next. She didn't have money for a taxi or a hotel room. It didn't matter. She just needed to get away.

She stepped out of the club and took a deep breath, inhaling the hot and humid air. A crowd of people was waiting to get into the club and the flashing lights from the sea of paparazzi cameras blinded her. She felt lightheaded as the emotions battled inside her. Her legs wobbled just as she felt Sebastian's hand wrap around her waist.

"Make me run after you again," he whispered against her ear, "and you will not like the consequences."

"That wasn't my plan," she said quietly. "And you will not like the consequences if you make me angry again."

"I believe the term is jealous," Sebastian said as he escorted her to his black limousine.

"I'm not jealous." Jealousy would mean that her emotions were involved. That it wasn't just sex between them. "I simply don't share."

"Neither do I," he warned.

"Where to, Mr. Cruz?" the chauffeur in the dark suit asked as he opened the door for them to enter the car.

"Home," Sebastian said.

Ashley shook her head. "I'm not getting in there with you." She sensed the chauffeur's surprise, but she didn't look at him. She knew it was a bold statement, when Sebastian could easily pick her up and toss her in the backseat. Considering the dark mood he was in, he might choose the trunk.

His hand flexed on her waist. "I'm not in the mood for a scene."

She felt the attention of the crowd and the flashing lights from the cameras were going fast and furious. She didn't want an audience, but she had to tell Sebastian exactly how she felt. "I told you that I don't play games," she said in a low voice, hoping no one could hear their conversation. "If you are going to spend the next month trying to make me jealous, we are going to end it here."

There was a long beat of tense silence before Sebastian spoke. "You're right. I shouldn't have done that and I'm not proud of it," he said begrudgingly. "I was trying to prove a point and it backfired."

Ashley didn't move or look at him. She knew this was as close as she was going to get to an apology but she needed more. He wasn't going to give it to her. It was best to end this now.

"It won't happen again," he said. "I promise."

She glanced up. She hadn't expected that from Sebastian. She stared into his eyes and saw the sincerity and regret. She didn't know if she should trust it. He could be lying. This could be a game to him. The man was a seducer. A womanizer.

But she wanted to believe him. And that's what scared her. She was willing to believe he would honor his promise when there was no proof that he would.

It was because she wanted to stay, she realized dazedly. Her body yearned for his touch and she knew she would regret it if she left. Sebastian had been correct; this agreement wasn't just about Inez Key. She wanted another chance to experience the exquisite and intense pleasure one more time.

Ashley gave a sharp nod and saw the sexual hunger flare in Sebastian's eyes. Excitement gripped her as she stepped into the limousine. She found it hard to breathe as her heart pounded in her ears. She was ready for whatever the night may bring.

But she would not surrender.

CHAPTER FIVE

ASHLEY SAT NEXT to Sebastian as the limousine slowly drove through the busy streets of Miami. The bright, colorful lights streamed through the dark windows. She stared at the tinted divider that separated them from the driver. She knew the chauffeur couldn't see or hear them. No one could. They were alone in a luxurious cocoon and the wait was agony.

The air crackled between them. The silence clawed at her. This was no longer lust. This was chemistry. Ashley knew Sebastian felt this dark magic between them.

She turned her head and greedily looked at Sebastian. She noticed every harsh angle in his face and the powerful lines of his gray suit. Her heart stopped for one painful moment when she saw his face tighten with desire.

"Ashley," Sebastian said huskily.

She rubbed her bare legs together and shivered when he said her name. It was a plea and a warning. He didn't want to wait any longer. Couldn't.

"Cruz," she said breathlessly. She blushed as she fought the overwhelming need to touch Sebastian and hold on to him. She took a sharp intake of breath and inhaled his clean, masculine scent. She felt the heat invade her body. She wanted to get closer and burrow her face into his skin.

"Call me Sebastian," he reminded her. He spoke softly, but she saw the glint in his eyes. He was the hunter and she was the prey. Ashley went very still, every instinct telling her he was about to pounce.

Instead, he reached for her hand. She felt a tremor in him as he raised her fingers to his mouth. A sense of power flooded her body. She was an average woman, young and with very little experience, but she could make the great Sebastian Cruz tremble.

"I want you right now." Sebastian brushed his mouth against her knuckles and her skin tingled from his touch. "But I know you're not ready. You need something more private before you lose control. Feel safe before you say exactly what you want."

He knew. He knew exactly how she felt. In his bed, she would go wild. It would be just the two of them. No interruption. No confined spaces. But here…in this limousine, on the crowded streets, she would be careful. She would be constantly aware of her surroundings.

Sebastian cupped her jaw with his hands. She felt surprisingly delicate under his large fingers. "You don't need to hold back with me."

"I'm not," she lied. She was cautious with everyone. She usually didn't act unless she knew the outcome. She didn't speak until she considered the consequences.

"I'll take care of you, *mi vida,*" he said in a low, clear voice.

Her heart gave a twist. She wanted to believe him. She wanted to believe that he cared more than this moment, more than the thrill of the hunt. That he cared about her. She would like to think he was the kind of man who viewed sex as something more than a sport.

But that wasn't a fairy tale she could afford to believe. "Do you tell that to all your women?" She tried to say it lightly, but she couldn't hide the cynical edge in her voice.

"I'm telling it to you," he said as he covered her mouth with his.

He kissed her and she immediately melted into him. She had dreamed about this moment every night since he had left Inez Key. She didn't realize how much she had yearned for his touch until now. But it wasn't enough. She needed more.

Sebastian's kiss was slow and tender. That wasn't what she wanted. She wanted to feel the heat and the passion from their first night. Ashley kissed Sebastian with abandon.

She poured everything she felt into the kiss and it was like touching a lit match to a firecracker. Something inside him broke free and Ashley tasted the wildness in his kiss. It excited her and she deepened the kiss, craving more.

"If you don't want this," he said roughly against her lips, "tell me now. This is your last chance to walk away."

Ashley was surprised that Sebastian was giving her an escape. Thanks to their agreement, he no longer had to seduce or romance her. She thought he would grab and take—and some part of her wished he would take the decision away from her. Then she couldn't blame herself for wanting this or enjoying his touch.

She wouldn't completely shatter here, in the back of a limo. No matter what he did, she wouldn't lose her inhibitions. Not when she felt as if they could get caught any moment.

Sebastian, however, didn't seem to be aware of their surroundings. Or he simply didn't care. This time, she could seduce him while he got lost in the sensations.

She was in full control and she was almost dizzy with the power. She knew she could ask for anything and he would give it to her. But she wanted something more. Ashley wanted—needed—Sebastian to surrender. She needed to see that he would do anything, give up control, just for the taste of her.

But how did one seduce a seducer? Could a man like Sebastian be seduced if he knew all the techniques and tricks? She knew she had to be daring. No fear. No hesitation.

Ashley deepened the kiss. She yanked off his tie and hastily unbuttoned his shirt. She stopped midway and flattened her hands against his warm skin. Sebastian moaned against her mouth as her fingertips tugged the dusting of dark curls on his chest.

She wanted more and shoved his jacket off and pulled his shirt down his arms. Tearing her mouth away from his, she kissed a trail down his chin and neck. She felt the choppy beat of his pulse and smiled as it matched hers.

Sebastian bunched her dress in his hands. She couldn't

strip bare for him. Not now. Not here. She stopped him, her hands firm against his. "Not yet," she mumbled against his chest.

"Are you telling me what to do?" he teased.

By the end of the night, he wouldn't notice that he was following her directions. He wouldn't care that she was in charge. Sebastian would only notice how she made him go wild. He would find out just how much power she had over him.

"I'm telling you to be patient," she corrected him as she grabbed his belt and pulled him closer. "Good things happen to those who wait."

"I have never found that to be true," he drawled.

She held his gaze steadily. "Trust me." The agreement didn't make them equals, but she needed his trust as much as she needed his touch.

Ashley was pleased when Sebastian reluctantly pulled his hands away from her dress and continued caressing her legs. Her fingers shook as they skimmed along his waist. Without taking her eyes off him, she slowly unbuckled his belt and pressed her hand against his erection. Her breath fizzled in her lungs when she realized how large and powerful he was. Her memory had not exaggerated.

"I'm not that patient," he warned as she rubbed her palm against him.

"Good to know." Her seduction was working. She had admired the restraint and patience he had displayed on Inez Key. It set him apart from the playboys she knew. Ashley knew he wasn't reckless or impulsive, but now she knew he had a limit.

But knowing his limit didn't make him any less dangerous. And right now *she* was feeling dangerous. She wasn't ready to stop this. She didn't think she could if she wanted to.

Ashley slowly unzipped his trousers and shoved them past his hips and down his legs. His hooded eyes glittered as he was sprawled half-naked before her. She couldn't stop staring at his masculine beauty.

"Now you." His voice was thick with desire as he reached for her.

She held up her hands. "Not yet." Ashley wasn't ready to give up the power that was rolling through her. She wanted to set the pace or he would take over. This would be the most brazen move she'd ever made.

She met his gaze as she wrapped her fingers around his thick penis. Sebastian hissed as she stroked him. She watched with fascination as he responded to her quickening pace. She felt his power underneath her skin and she wanted more of it.

Ashley knelt down in front of Sebastian and took him in her mouth. His deep moan echoed in the interior of the car as he clenched his hands into her hair. She loved the taste of him, loved driving him wild. She enjoyed the bite of pain as he twisted her hair in his fists and she welcomed his thrusts.

Just when she thought she was going to take him over the edge, Sebastian pulled away. She murmured her protest when he lifted her. She wasn't going to let him take this away from her. Not now, not when she found the courage to take charge.

Ashley pushed Sebastian back in the seat and

climbed on top of him. She straddled his hips and met his hot gaze. He didn't look smug or arrogant anymore. He looked wild, almost savage.

She felt beautiful. Confident. She had the man who had invaded her dreams and taken over every waking moment underneath her. He was at her mercy.

"Wait," he said in a growl as he reached for his wallet and retrieved a condom. As he tossed his wallet aside and slid on the condom with quick, efficient moves, Ashley realized he was nowhere near to losing control. He had the sense to remember protection and it had slipped her mind. Was she fooling herself, believing she was in charge?

Ashley placed her palms on his broad shoulders just as he clenched his hands on her hips and guided her down. The heat washed over her. She tossed back her head and moaned as he filled her.

The sensations were almost too intense. She rocked her hips as the pleasure rippled through her. Sebastian leaned forward and captured her breast with his mouth. She begged for more, her words broken and jumbled, as the heat flared deep in her pelvis.

He cupped her bottom and squeezed as he murmured his encouragement in Spanish. She didn't catch all the words. She rocked harder, chasing the pleasure that she didn't quite understand. Couldn't quite curb. But she wasn't scared because she knew Sebastian would take care of her. He wouldn't let her go too close to the fire and burn.

Sebastian grabbed her hips and controlled the rhythm. She could barely catch her breath. She saw the muscle bunching in his clenched jaw. She saw the lust glittering in his dark eyes. He was desperate to hold on to the remnants of his control. He wanted to be the last to let go.

Ashley wasn't going to let that happen. She was in charge. She would make him beg for release and she would decide if she would give it to him.

Sebastian slid his hand to where they were joined. He pressed his fingertip on her clitoris and Ashley stilled. She arched back and groaned as the climax ripped through her body. Her mind went blank as she surrendered to the white heat.

"Sebastian!" His name ripped from her throat. Ashley slumped against him, her muscles weak and pulsating, as she heard his short cry of release.

So this is how it feels to be a rich man's plaything, Ashley thought as she lay in bed hours later, naked and spent. Sebastian was curled next to her, his arm wrapped around her waist. Even in his sleep, he made his claim known.

She was now a mistress. A sigh staggered from Ashley's throat as she looked at the moon through the windows. The one thing she swore she'd never become.

Ashley knew she should be filled with shame and self-hatred. She should feel as if a piece of her soul had been stolen. Instead, she felt protected. Taken care of. Cherished.

Was this how her mother felt when she had been a mistress? Was this why Linda designed her life around

Donald? Why she suddenly came alive every time he stepped into the room?

No, her mother had it much worse, Ashley realized. Linda made the mistake of falling in love with her benefactor.

Ashley turned and looked at Sebastian while he slept. She wouldn't make that mistake. She may desire Sebastian, she may even be infatuated with him, but she would not fall in love. If she did that, she'd never recover.

Hours later Ashley dived into the crystal-blue infinity pool that was on the rooftop of Sebastian's penthouse apartment. The water felt cold and refreshing against her skin. The pool was designed for lazy afternoons under the hot sun, but Ashley swam down the length as hard and as fast as she could.

She loved the water. Whenever she was upset or worried, she found peace watching the waves or swimming laps. But today, nothing could calm her.

Ashley tried to exhaust herself as she thought about what had happened in the limousine. And the wild, fierce sex they'd had when Sebastian carried her to bed. And this morning…

She felt her skin flush. Reaching the edge of the pool, Ashley did a turn and kept swimming. She was becoming a sexual creature and there were no signs that she could pull back. She needed to return to Inez Key before she got to the point of no return.

Ashley paused when she heard a splash. She stopped

swimming and started to tread water. Looking around, she saw Sebastian swimming toward her.

Her stomach tightened as she watched his clean, powerful strokes. She couldn't deny his strength and masculinity. Ashley couldn't stop staring. She was tempted to jump out of the pool before she wrapped her body around his.

Instead, she remained treading water, refusing to give an inch, watching him approach with a mix of dread and excitement. When he surfaced, she immediately thought that he was too close. She saw the amused gleam in his dark eyes.

"I thought you were at work," she said. She had been grateful for the time alone. She was used to solitude and thought the time away from Sebastian would help break this sexual hold he had over her. No such luck. She only had to look at him and she was right back where she started. Her pulse kicked with excitement as she savored the heat sizzling through her veins.

"I came back because I wanted to see you," he replied as his gaze settled on her skimpy bikini top.

Knowing that she had the ability to distract him from work gave her more joy than it should. He probably tossed these meaningless comments to every woman in his sight. "I found this swimsuit in the cabana," she said as she slicked back her wet hair. "There were quite a few of them."

"They are there for guests," he said, moving even closer. "They are not from my ex-lovers, if that's what you're thinking."

Her insecurity was pathetically obvious. She hated

what she was becoming. "If you say so." She realized he had moved in even closer. Ashley couldn't take it anymore and slowly moved to the corner of the pool.

"Where are you going?" With one smooth move, Sebastian cornered her. She felt the edge of the pool against her back and Sebastian's strong legs bumping against hers.

Her hands grazed his defined chest as she tried to tread. "My God, you are insatiable."

Sebastian rested his hands on the pool ledge, trapping her. "You were the one who woke me up this morning. Not that I minded..."

She didn't want to think about that. How she acted before she thought. She couldn't even use the excuse that she had been dreaming. That would make Sebastian more arrogant than he already was.

Ashley treaded hard and fast with her legs but she was getting tangled with Sebastian's. She was very aware of his body. His solid chest and golden-brown skin. The strong column of his throat and his sensual mouth.

Sebastian bent his head and kissed her. She arched her back as his hand slid down the curve of her breast. Ashley moaned as he rubbed his thumb against her hard nipple.

"I have a favor to ask," she said breathlessly.

"I can't wait to hear it." He dipped his head and whispered in her ear, "You don't have to be shy with me."

"I need to visit Inez Key," she said in a rush.

"No." His quiet, authoritative tone bothered her almost as much as his words.

She reared back her head. "What do you mean, no? Aren't you the least bit curious of why I need to go?"

He shrugged. "You have no authority on or responsibility to the island. It's mine."

"Shouldn't I at least get bonus points for asking?" She realized what she'd said and shook her head. Why was she asking for permission? If she wanted to go, she would. Thanks to a very informative phone conversation with Clea, Ashley knew Sebastian had added security on Inez Key. But she knew all the best hiding spots.

Sebastian's mouth formed into a grim line. "Don't even think about it."

"You don't know what I'm thinking," she said as she hoisted herself out of the pool.

"I'll arrest you for trespassing."

All right, he did know what she was thinking. Was her face that expressive? Or was she just predictable? "You'll have to catch me first," Ashley said as she strolled away. She refused to show how much she believed he would follow through on his threat.

"You won't get far," Sebastian said as he watched her from the pool.

Yes, she would. Ashley grabbed her towel and walked as regally as she could back to the penthouse. She was painfully aware of Sebastian watching her. Her skin felt hot and tight and her hips seemed fuller as they swayed with each step. She waited until she was out of sight before she wrapped her towel tightly around her body and ran down the steps as if she was being pursued.

CHAPTER SIX

A WEEK LATER, Ashley strolled from one guest to another at Sebastian's glamorous cocktail party. They were on the rooftop of the Cruz hotel in Jamaica. The breeze carried the scent of the ocean and the tropical-fruit appetizers the waiters offered.

Ashley wasn't sure why she'd quietly assumed the role as hostess. She could say that she was bored or that she rebelled from Sebastian's attempts to keep her away from the party. The truth was she wanted to show him that she was more than just decoration. She had some skills that weren't marketable but still valued in certain circles.

If Sebastian suspected that she would sabotage him, she hoped he realized he had no cause for concern. She knew how to act, what to provide and how to dress. Ashley's skin was bare of jewels, but her simple white dress made her stand out from the dark suits and frilly and colorful dresses.

More important, she made sure everyone felt comfortable and welcome. She knew this party changed the way Sebastian saw her. She saw the admiration and pride in his eyes.

"I thought you didn't like parties," Sebastian said as she made her way to him.

"When did I say that?" Ashley asked. She tilted her head as she tried to remember. "No, I said I didn't party. No late nights. No club hopping. Nothing like that."

Sebastian didn't try to hide his skepticism. "Not even in college? You had only been there for one semester."

"And you think I got kicked out of school?" What made him think that? She had done some dumb things when she was a teenager, but she wasn't a troublemaker. "No, I was struggling at school. I always had trouble with my grades. I dropped out after my parents died. I didn't see the point in staying."

She'd never wanted to go to school. Her parents forced her for their selfish reasons, but she had to admit that college offered her a respite from the tension at home.

"If you were such a poor student, how did you get into college?"

"My father pulled some strings and gave a big donation to the school," she admitted with the twist of her lips.

Sebastian raised his eyebrows. "Must have been nice to have rich parents," he said coldly. "They opened a lot of doors and gave you many opportunities."

"That wasn't why they did it," Ashley said as she tightly gripped the stem of her champagne flute tightly. "They wanted me out of the way. But I know what you're saying. I was given a lot. I had the resources to make something of myself. And where did I wind up? Broke, homeless and a rich man's sexual plaything."

Sebastian's eyes narrowed. "You twist my words."

She knew what he was saying. Really saying. That he could have conquered the world by now with that kind of financial support. "You may have had to crawl out of the ghetto but I'm sure someone helped you," Ashley said roughly. "Teachers, neighbors, relatives. Maybe the kindness of strangers."

"Then you would be wrong."

Ashley felt her heart pinch. Sebastian had had a grueling and lonely journey to the top. She couldn't imagine the strength and sacrifice it took to get to where he was. The more she learned about him, the more she admired and respected him. It made it difficult keeping her distance from Sebastian.

"And what about now?" she asked, deciding to take a different tack. "I'm sure that you would do exactly what my father did. If one of your sisters needed to get into a school, get a job or even a place to live, you would throw all of your money and influence to get it for her."

Something flickered in his eyes, but his face showed no expression. She watched Sebastian take a healthy gulp of champagne. "Yes, I would."

"And she would accept that help," Ashley predicted. "That doesn't make her spoiled."

"Of course not. I expect my sisters to come to me whenever they need help."

"But I'm a spoiled brat because I lived off my parents' money?" she asked. "You think I haven't worked a day in my life. That I'm just hanging around, working on my tan, until I land a rich husband."

"Are you trying to tell me that you aren't an heiress who enjoyed the good life," he asked.

"I once enjoyed being a socialite when I didn't have to worry about money or the future," she admitted. The amount of money she had wasted in those years still made her sick to her stomach. "But that disappeared the moment my mother pulled a gun on my father. My friends used their connection with me to sell the most salacious and untrue stories about my family. My father's money was gone and I inherited a mess. It has been a struggle for five years to keep what I had left."

"You could have gotten a job," he drawled.

She should have expected that she would receive no sympathy from Sebastian. "I couldn't leave Inez Key. Everyone thinks I've been living in paradise. No one wants to look past the island and notice that I've been living hand to mouth for years. Any money I had went to taxes or to the islanders who relied on me."

"If your home has been such a headache, why are you so desperate to go back?"

Ashley pressed her lips together. She had been trying to prove a point, but Sebastian only noticed the one thing she had been trying to hide. "You wouldn't understand," she muttered.

"Try me."

She looked away as she struggled with the urge to tell him everything. Why did she start this? Why was it so important for Sebastian to see her as something more than a pampered heiress? His opinion shouldn't matter so much.

"Inez Key is the only place where I feel safe." She

knew she'd told him that before but she wasn't willing to explain why. That she wasn't destructive or cruel when she was on the island. That she didn't have the ability to destroy people's lives and families if she disconnected with the world.

Sebastian's face darkened. "Do you feel unsafe now?" he asked hoarsely as his eyes glittered. "Here, with me?"

She didn't feel unsafe. She was scared. Worried of how addicted she was to Sebastian's touch. Afraid of the emotions whipping through her. Frightened of what she was becoming. A sexual woman. Emotional. Falling in love.

"You've enjoyed yourself the past couple of weeks," Sebastian stated. "And why not? Private planes, designer clothes and state-of-the-art spa services. We've been to the Bahamas, the Cayman Islands and now Jamaica. You've stayed at the most luxurious resorts that would put Inez Key to shame."

And he thought it was all because of the money he spent? Let him think that. If he knew she enjoyed his company, his attention and his touch, it would give him far too much power over her.

She had been amazed that Sebastian had taken time out of his busy schedule to show her the sights. He had taken her everyplace she had underlined in her travel guide, but he had also taken her to his favorite spots. She had cherished those moments as they offered her a deeper understanding about Sebastian Cruz.

"Is that why you dragged me along on your business

trip?" she asked coolly. "So I would see what the world outside Inez Key had to offer?"

"You don't seem to mind. Your every need has been catered to."

She had made the most of what he had to offer. It reminded her of what she used to take for granted. No wonder he thought she was a spoiled socialite. Little did he know that she'd had a makeover and subjected herself to the most painful spa services for his approval.

It was only later when she realized that she was following her mother's pattern. She could tell herself that she chose bright colors because it reflected her mood. That the mane of hair was easier to deal with and the short dresses were needed in the tropical heat. It wasn't true. It was all to please Sebastian.

Not that it mattered. He didn't seem to notice her haircut or her smooth skin. The lingerie she wore was for his pleasure as much as it was for hers, but he managed to get it off her before he gave it an appreciative look.

"And your needs are catered to especially in bed," he murmured.

Ashley blushed. She wasn't quiet about what she wanted in bed. The nights they shared had been mind-blowing. She had never expected that it would become more magical. She clung to Sebastian all night, eager and greedy for his touch.

"I have no complaints," she replied stiffly. She wondered how amazing it would be if Sebastian had any emotion behind every caress and kiss. Her knees weakened at the thought.

"Nor do I," he whispered as he leaned forward. "You are a very generous lover."

Her face felt incredibly hot from his compliment and the noise from the cocktail party seemed louder. She never refused Sebastian and it had nothing to do with her role as his mistress. She was always ready for him at the most inconvenient times. Even now her breasts felt heavy, her nipples tight, as her skin tingled for his caress.

But she didn't have that power over him. Sebastian wanted her but only on his terms. His timetable.

"If you will excuse me," she said as she forced herself to step away. They were not equals and they never would be. "I'm not being a good hostess. I should circulate with your guests."

Impatience gleamed in his eyes. "Running away again, *mi vida?*"

She didn't answer and she walked away. Ashley felt his gaze on her. She knew she couldn't hide from Sebastian Cruz. He saw everything.

Sebastian fought the impulse to grab Ashley and pull her closer. To find a dark corner and reacquaint himself with her scent and taste. Instead, he restrained himself as he watched the haughty tilt of her head as she glided through the crowd.

Ashley may think she was an island girl but she was meant for the glittery world of high society. She had nothing in common with the guests, but she worked the room with effortless grace. The businessmen were dazzled by her friendly smile and their wives gravitated to her sunny personality.

"Who's the girl?"

Sebastian's hand tightened on his champagne glass when he heard the gravelly voice. He turned to see Oscar Salazar, one of his fiercest rivals.

"Salazar." He gave the man a brief handshake. "I didn't see you come in."

"Your attention was elsewhere. I can see why." A streak of red highlighted Salazar's blunt cheekbones as he stared at Ashley. "You always had good taste in property."

"Don't let her hear you say that," Sebastian warned. Not that he was going to allow Salazar that close to Ashley. He was territorial, but he knew better than to show it around Salazar. The man liked to compete. The more Sebastian wanted something, the more determined Salazar was in wrestling it free from him.

The possessive feeling was so strong that Sebastian almost vibrated with it. He couldn't remember the last time he'd felt this way. The women in his bed had always been interchangeable and temporary. If any of them tried to make him jealous, Sebastian didn't hesitate to cut them loose. He never second-guessed or regretted his actions. He knew he could replace his lover with someone who was willing to follow his rules.

But it was different with Ashley. The woman didn't understand the word *obey*. She was exasperating, difficult and never boring. Why did he allow her to act that way? Was it because she was his mistress? Was it because he was her first? Or did it have anything to do with sex?

He wanted to share his day with Ashley. It didn't matter if they were exploring the waterfalls of Jamaica, falling asleep in each other's arms or enjoying a cup of coffee in a busy sidewalk café. He yearned for her. So much that he found himself calling her when he was at the office just to hear her voice.

"Who did you say she was?" Salazar asked as his gaze narrowed on Ashley's slender body.

Sebastian gritted his teeth. He had to play this carefully. "Her name is Ashley."

"She looks familiar."

He doubted Salazar socialized with Donald Jones. He was too young and had only made his fortune a few years ago. "You probably saw her in Miami," Sebastian said. He tossed back the champagne but didn't taste it.

Salazar dragged his gaze away from Ashley. "She's different from your other women."

And that automatically made her an intriguing challenge. The ultimate prize. The man understood what made Sebastian tick. "I don't have a type."

Salazar smiled. "This one looks more innocent. Untamed."

Sebastian curled his hand into a fist. "You don't know anything about her." *And you're not going to*.

"But I know you," Salazar said. "You'll tire of her very soon."

No, he wouldn't. He wanted more than a month with Ashley. Craved for something more. "And you'll swoop in and catch her?"

Salazar shrugged. "I wouldn't normally take your hand-me-downs…"

Sebastian wanted to punch his rival. No one talked about Ashley that way. *No one*. Instead, Sebastian stepped in front of Salazar and stared him down. "Stay away from Ashley," he said in growl.

Salazar looked very pleased that he'd riled him. "Worried that you don't have that much of a hold on her?" he taunted.

He *was* worried about that. The only way he got Ashley back in his bed was through blackmail. He wasn't proud of it. She wanted him but not enough to make the first move or accept his original offer.

"She's mine," Sebastian warned in a low voice. Most people would scatter from the threat in his tone, but Oscar Salazar's smile only widened.

"Not for long." Salazar returned his gaze on Ashley. "I could steal her away if I wanted to."

"No, you couldn't." Sebastian's heart pounded against his ribs as the need to defend his territory coursed through his veins. "You have nothing she wants. No extra incentive."

"Incentive?" Salazar's eyes glowed as he pondered the new information. "She has a price?"

"One you couldn't afford," Sebastian snapped.

"I'm sure I could get a bargain," he murmured.

"You've been warned, Salazar." He didn't like this side of him, but he couldn't stop it. He was ready to unleash all of his power and weapons on Salazar. If he had fangs, he would have bared them. "Go anywhere near her and you're dead."

"Understood." Salazar took a sip of his champagne and casually strolled away. Sebastian wanted to follow, but one of his Jamaican business partners chose that moment to approach.

Sebastian ruthlessly pushed aside any thought of Salazar. His blood roared in his ears and his hands shook with the need to land his fist into Salazar's jaw. He had nothing to worry about. He didn't trust the man, but he knew Ashley wouldn't be interested in Salazar's questionable charms.

Yet he kept an eye on Ashley during the cocktail party. Sebastian was always aware of where she stood. Even when he was in a deep conversation with his executive assistant, Sebastian heard Ashley's earthy laugh from across the room.

He wasn't sure what made him look up a few minutes later and actively seek her out in the party. His mother would have called it a premonition. Sebastian knew it had more to do with the fact that he was attuned to her.

He found her next to the door on the rooftop. The ocean breeze tugged at her white dress and her long brown hair. His voice trailed off as he noticed that Ashley stood ramrod straight. Her tension was palpable. Her polite smile was slipping and he saw the caution in her eyes.

It took him a moment to realize Oscar Salazar had his back to the party and was talking to her. A red haze filled Sebastian's vision as the anger flared inside him. He strode through the crowd, determined to keep Salazar away. He didn't notice the guests as he bumped shoulders and cut through small groups. A few guests saw the murderous rage in his expression and immediately got out of the line of fire.

He didn't know what Salazar was saying to Ashley, but it didn't matter. Ashley was *his*. Body and soul.

He saw Ashley's face whiten. The color leached from her sun-kissed skin as if she was going to be sick. She turned her head and Sebastian knew she was searching for him. Their gazes clashed. Her brown eyes shimmered with hurt. Pain. Betrayal.

Ashley flinched and jerked her attention back at Salazar. Ashley's mouth parted in shock a moment before she slung her champagne in Salazar's face. She dropped the flute on the ground and marched away before Salazar could react.

Sebastian wanted to chase after his woman. Comfort and protect her. But first he had to take care of Salazar. He turned and glared at Salazar's proud face. That man needed to learn that if he slighted Ashley, the wrath of hell was upon him.

Ashley brushed away the last tear as she gathered up her T-shirt and jeans and dumped them in the smallest suitcase she could find. Her hands shook as she zipped up the case. How could Sebastian do this to her?

Why was she so surprised? She meant nothing to him. She was just the mistress. A very temporary one. Hadn't she seen enough on how men treated their mistresses? Why did she think Sebastian would have been any different?

Ashley jumped when she heard the door of their bedroom swing open and bang against the wall. She refused to look at Sebastian. She knew he filled the doorway with his hands clutching the frame. He was barring her exit and she felt his anger pouring through him.

"What happened between you and Salazar?" he asked with lethal softness.

"Bastard," she muttered as she lifted the suitcase off the bed.

"He's been called much worse, but what did he say to you?" Sebastian asked impatiently. "I couldn't get a word out of him."

"No, you are the bastard," Ashley said as she thrust a finger at him. He looked like a dark angel. He had discarded his jacket and tie, but that didn't diminish his raw masculinity. There was something angry and volatile about him. Dangerous and powerful. "I trusted you. I thought we had an agreement."

"We do," he said as he stepped into the room. "You are my mistress for a month."

"Which you told Oscar Salazar." Her voice shook as she remembered the way that man had looked at her. As if he wanted to sample the goods before he made a bid.

"I didn't say you were my mistress." Sebastian's voice was as stinging as the flick of a whip. "I warned him off."

Then how did Oscar know? She didn't act like a mistress. She didn't dress like one, either. The only way he would have known was if Sebastian said something. "You broke your promise and you broke our agreement. I'm leaving."

"Like hell you are." Sebastian rushed forward. He

grabbed the case and tossed it on the floor. "You're not going anywhere until I say so."

She'd never seen Sebastian like this. His movements were rough and clumsy. His sophisticated veneer was slipping. It was as if he was upset that she was leaving. But that was ridiculous. Sebastian Cruz didn't care enough to panic.

Ashley thrust out her chin and met his gaze. "You can't tell me what to do. I'm not your mistress anymore."

A muscle bunched in his jaw. "Then you will never see Inez Key again."

"Fine," she retorted. She pressed her lips together as the horror snaked through her. She wanted to take those words back.

His eyes widened with surprise. He was silent for a moment, his breathing hard, as a strange urgency pulsed around them. "Fine? You are ready to walk away from the home you fought to hold on to?" he asked as he stepped closer. "The home you took care of and made sacrifices for? The one where you lowered yourself and slept with me so you could stay on the island?"

"This isn't about Inez Key. It's about you," she replied. "You don't care about what is important to me and you certainly don't care about my feelings."

He rocked back on his feet as he looked at her with such intensity that she felt she was going to burst. "How are you going to get back?" he asked. "You have no money."

Ashley closed her eyes as the pain ricocheted inside her. He didn't deny her accusation. He didn't care about her feelings. "I don't know," she whispered. "I'll hock this dress. I'll swim all the way home. Maybe I'll trade my body for favors. That's what everyone thinks I do anyway."

He snatched her wrist. She felt the tremor in his hand. "Don't even joke about it."

"Why not, Sebastian?" She tried to yank her arm away from him but he tightened his hold. "You made me a joke. You made me a mistress."

"And you accepted," he said. "You had other choices. You could have walked away but you didn't."

"You dangled my home as bait," she cried out.

"Like you said, Inez Key had nothing to do with it," he reminded her coldly. "You wanted to be with me but you were afraid to go after it. And now you're upset because you like being a mistress."

Her gasp echoed in the room as she went still. "No, I don't," she said in a scandalized whisper. "Take that back."

"I stand corrected." Sebastian let go of her wrist. "You like being *my* mistress."

She wanted to slap him. Push him away. But it was true. She liked sharing his bed and enjoyed seeing the desire in his eyes when she walked into the room. She treasured their private moments and was proud to be at his side in public. She ached for his touch and she was greedy for his undivided attention. She would accept whatever role he chose for her if it meant she could share a part of his life.

And he knew it. He knew that she would take the

measly crumbs that he offered. He knew he had that much power over her. "Get out of my way."

He crossed his arms and braced his feet. Any concern he felt a moment ago had disappeared. Sebastian was calm and in charge again. "Make me."

And now he was going to prove how she had no power over him. Ashley curled her hands into fists and dug her nails into her palms as she tried to hold back the rioting emotions. "I'm warning you, Sebastian. I'm about to lose control."

Sebastian wasn't worried. "I can handle it. Give me your best shot."

"Oh, my God." She thrust her hands in her wavy hair. "You *want* me out of control? Are you insane?"

"I want you to stop hiding. Stop running away."

That was all she wanted to do. Run. Hide. Regain control of her temper before she broke into a million pieces. "You have no say in what I do."

"I'm sorry about Salazar," he said grimly. "I warned him off but I revealed more than I should."

"Did you tell him I had a price?" she asked wildly. "That he could talk me down from my asking price because I was damaged goods? That I should accept his offer because you would kick me out of your bed soon?"

"I'm going to kill him," Sebastian said through clenched teeth.

"You'll have to get in line," she declared as she strode to the door. "I knew I shouldn't have trusted you, Sebastian. I respected your wishes but you didn't respect mine."

Sebastian was at the threshold before she could get there and slammed the door shut. "You are not leaving."

She reached for the doorknob. "I see no reason to stay."

"What about this?" he asked as his hands covered her shoulders.

It was the only warning she had before Sebastian turned her around and covered his mouth with hers. His kiss crushed her lips. Ashley pressed her hands against his chest, determined to push him away. He ignored her attempts as he settled her against the door.

Excitement burned through her. She shouldn't want this. Shouldn't encourage it. Yet she did want it, had waited for this moment. Ashley wanted to feel his hands shake with barely restrained emotion. She wanted the last of his control to snap and show exactly what was going through his mind.

Sebastian shoved her lace panties down her hips before he lifted her up. She wrapped her legs around his waist when he yanked her dress up her thighs. As he deepened the kiss, Ashley tore at his shirt, wanting to strip it from his body.

Sebastian groaned against her swollen lips. "Tell me you don't want this."

She wished she could. She wished she didn't come alive under his touch or that she was always waiting, yearning, for his kiss. Ashley bucked her hips, silently demanding more.

Sebastian whispered something in Spanish as he shucked his trousers off. She couldn't tell if it was a prayer or a curse. She clung to his shoulders, yielding to his fierce kisses, unable to deny him anything. Desire and anger coiled deep in her belly, hot and tight. It was a potent combination. A dangerous mix.

Ashley tensed when she felt the crown of his penis pressing against her. She hated herself for wanting this. Hated that she made it so easy for him. She tilted her hips as he drove into her welcoming heat.

She turned her head and moaned as he filled her. Ashley held on to Sebastian tightly as he thrust deep. His rhythm was ferocious and wild. She couldn't get enough. The sounds of their uneven breaths and the creaking door were harsh to her ears. The scent of hot, aroused male electrified the air. She clutched to his fine cotton shirt as she rocked her hips against him.

"Walk away and you'll never feel like this again," he declared gruffly as he burrowed his head against the base of her throat. His teeth nipped her skin as if he was leaving his brand.

Ashley knew he was right. Only Sebastian had this power over her. The sexual hunger clawed inside her. It was unbearable, pressing against her, demanding to break free.

"You will always be mine."

Ashley's sobs caught in her throat as the violent climax ripped through her. She sagged against him as he continued to thrust. She couldn't fight the truth anymore. When he discarded her and moved on to another woman, she would still long for his touch.

She surrendered to the knowledge that she would always be his.

* * *

Sebastian woke up to the sound of his cell phone. He reached for the bedside table, his hands fumbling, but he couldn't find it. Blinking his eyes open, he immediately noticed two things: it was daylight and Ashley wasn't curled against him.

The silence in the hotel suite indicated that he was alone. Ashley was probably sulking. Angry that he'd proved his claim on her once and for all. He rolled out of bed and stalked naked to where he had shed his clothes the night before. He grabbed his cell phone from the pile of clothes and saw that his assistant was calling him.

"What is it?" he asked abruptly.

"I just found out that Ashley left Jamaica."

He hunched his shoulders as the news slammed against him. He'd made his claim and it had scared her off. She'd waited until he'd fallen asleep before she'd sneaked out of his bed. "How?" His voice was raspy and low.

"I heard a rumor," his assistant said nervously. "I don't have verification at the moment."

Sebastian closed his eyes as he got a bad feeling. He knew Ashley was angry with him, but she wouldn't betray him. Not like this. "Where is she?"

"With Oscar Salazar," his assistant whispered. "She's on his private plane back to Miami."

CHAPTER SEVEN

THE SUN STREAKED across the morning sky as Ashley saw a glimpse of Inez Key. The wind was cold and all she wore was a T-shirt, jeans and boat shoes. She didn't care. Her bottom lip quivered and the emotions crashed through her. She was home.

Home. She studied the antebellum mansion as she considered the word. It didn't feel like home anymore. Was it because it was time for her to move on or because she knew Sebastian owned it?

She knew she didn't belong here. Not because she was trespassing, and not because she'd ruined any chance of staying on as caretaker. There was no way Sebastian would allow her back now that she'd broken her promise.

But she didn't use Inez Key as just a home. It had been her hideaway. She had stayed here after her parents' murder-suicide because it was a safe place. She could evade prying eyes and evade living life.

Ashley knew she had been a lot like her mother and that scared her. She had an all-or-nothing attitude like Linda Valdez. Passionate about her causes, extremely loyal to her friends, and a hot temper that took years for her to control. Ashley knew how to hold on to a grudge and her friend's enemies were her enemies. It was only a matter of time before she followed in her mother's footsteps. To love completely and unwisely. To destroy and self-destruct.

Ashley thought she had escaped from that future when she hid away on Inez Key. It was paradise and yet solitary confinement. Her wild temper disappeared and her passions quieted. She was still fiercely loyal, but she wasn't consumed by love. She thought she'd broken the cycle and become the woman she wanted to be. But one night with Sebastian and Ashley realized she had only been fooling herself.

Ashley closed her eyes as the bleakness swirled inside her. She didn't want to think about that. Not now. First, she needed to step onto the beach and let the sand trickle between her toes. Then she needed to lie down and let the quiet wash over her. She would watch the view of the Atlantic Ocean and find the familiar landmarks. It could take hours before she felt whole and strong again. Days. But it would happen and then she would figure out what to do next.

Ashley struggled with exhaustion as she stepped out of the water taxi and paid the captain. It took effort to smile and give her thanks. She walked along the wooden dock, but she didn't feel like her old self. Everything felt new and different. She was different and she would never recapture the old Ashley Jones again.

She heard the boat speed away, but she didn't look back. The changes on the island had her attention. She noticed the repairs on the house and the fresh coat of paint. The wild vegetation was tamed. Inez Key was slowly returning to its former glory.

Unlike her. She was breaking down. Breaking apart. Even though she was finally back on Inez Key, she had to keep it together. She sensed that this island could no longer contain her.

Ashley walked to the front door of the main house and tried to open it. To her surprise, it was locked. She frowned and jiggled the doorknob. That was odd. Inez Key was a quiet and safe place with just a few homes and buildings. No one locked their doors. She couldn't remember the last time she'd used the key or where she had left it.

"Ashley, is that you?" Clea asked as she walked from around the house. She gave a squeal and ran to Ashley, welcoming her with a big hug. "What are you doing back?"

"I was going to get my things and leave," Ashley said as she gestured to the door. "But the main house is locked."

"I know, isn't that strange? Who locks their doors?" Clea asked. She planted her fists on her hips and shook her head. "I haven't been in there since they started renovating."

"A lot has changed." She gave a nod at the tropical flowers and plants near the white columns. At first glance the landscaping looked natural, but she knew it had been meticulously planned. How did Sebastian manage all of the changes when the island had only recently been in possession? "I wasn't gone that long."

"The new owners have been busy," Clea said as she guided Ashley away from the front door. "And there are a lot of new security features. It won't be long before the guards find you."

"They haven't torn anything down," Ashley murmured as she gave the main house one last look.

"It's more like adding and updating," Clea said. "I'm glad to see they have respect for the history of the island, but I think the way of life on Inez Key won't be the same."

The gentle rhythm of the island life would change if there were bodyguards and security features. "Have you heard from the new owners?"

"We received letters from Cruz Conglomerate," the housekeeper said as they walked along a dusty path. "I thought it was going to be an eviction letter like yours, but they promised nothing has changed for us."

At least Sebastian didn't break that promise. She had suspected it was a threat to keep her in line, but she couldn't be sure. "What else did the letter say? Anything about turning the island into a resort or a hotel?" Or worse, razing it and destroying it inch by inch. Ashley shuddered at the thought.

She didn't think Sebastian would do that, but she obviously couldn't predict his every move. She suspected he wanted Inez Key for an exclusive getaway. He had undoubtedly posed as a paying guest to see if buying the island was worth his time.

And after spending a few weeks with the man, she noticed his interests focused on travel and leisure. She had stayed at some extraordinary hotels and exclusive resorts. All of them were part of his global business. Her home was definitely going to be part of that. The crowning jewel of his empire.

"No, I haven't heard what they plan to do with Inez Key," Clea said without a hint of concern. "We're expecting to see the new owner next month after the renovations are complete."

"You've already met the new owner," Ashley said bitterly. She hated how her voice caught in her throat. "You know him as Sebastian Esteban."

Clea halted and stared at Ashley. "That man took your island from you? The man you fell in love with?"

She shifted her lower jaw as she fought back the spurt of anger. "I did not fall in love with Sebastian Cruz."

"Honey, I saw how you were with him," Clea argued with a knowing smile. "You were in full bloom every time he looked at you."

Ashley closed her eyes as her skin heated. She couldn't be in love with Sebastian. She had more pride than that! The man had kicked her out of her home, made her his mistress and ruined her life.

But she couldn't hide from the truth anymore. She had been enthralled by Sebastian Cruz. It was more than the sizzling sexual hunger. Ashley didn't want to admire his hard-earned accomplishments or value his opinions. She tried not to help him or smile at his humor. She hid the longing for Sebastian's company and the way her heart leaped every time he entered the room.

None of it worked. No matter how hard she had tried, she had fallen for a man who had no respect for her. He only wanted her for sex.

It was official. She had inherited the same self-destructive tendencies as her mother.

"I'll get over it," Ashley muttered.

Clea patted Ashley's arm. "What are you going to do to get the island back?"

The question caught her by surprise. She had given up that plan weeks ago. "Nothing. I've done everything in my power." And discovered she was no match for Sebastian. "The most I could get out of Sebastian was the caretaker position, but I managed to mess that up."

"Caretaker? The owner of the island becoming a hired hand? I don't think so! Just as well you didn't get that job," Clea said with the cluck of her tongue. "You'll think of something. In the meantime, stay with Louis and me. Just for a couple of days."

The offer was tempting but Ashley hesitated. "I don't want to get you in trouble. He made it very clear I had to have his permission to stay on Inez Key. If he knew I was staying with you…"

Clea curled her arm around Ashley's. "Don't worry about him," she said in a conspiring tone. "He'll never know you were here."

Where was she? Icy anger swirled inside Sebastian as he strode across the beach on Inez Key the next evening. He curled his shoulders as the cold ocean breeze pulled at his jeans and hoodie. He didn't notice the colorful birds flitting from one flower to the next. The sound of rolling waves faded in the background. There was only one thing on his mind: finding Ashley.

He couldn't believe she would have pulled a stunt

like that. It was bad enough she had left his bed in the middle of the night, but to escape with Salazar? His anger flared white-hot. She was going to pay for that.

Didn't she know that he would follow her? Or was that the plan all along? Was Ashley determined to prove her sexual power? Her hold on him had been obvious on their last night in Jamaica.

He had chased her back to Miami and invaded Salazar's kingdom only to discover she wasn't there. Salazar had had great fun at his expense. Sebastian's anger had been a slow burn until the other man made one too many innuendos. The guy was no longer laughing and Sebastian hoped he'd left a scar. It would be a daily reminder to Salazar not to come near his woman.

Sebastian hated the fact that he had been compelled to chase Ashley. She made this decision. She chose to give up her last chance to stay on this island.

But he couldn't turn back now. When he first heard she'd left, he had been numb. It took a split second for the fury to crack through his frozen shell and drive him into action. The need to follow had been instinctive and strong. He seized upon it, not caring what his colleagues thought.

He had no strategy. He wasn't looking ahead. That wasn't how he operated, but Sebastian was working on pure rage. His anger had festered as he spent hours searching for her in Miami.

Sebastian let the anger swell inside him, ready to burst through his skin. Ashley Jones was a spoiled princess and he was going to teach her a lesson.

But where was she?

She had to be here. Sebastian ignored the panic squeezing his chest. If she wasn't in Inez Key, he had no idea where she would be.

Sebastian stopped and looked around. The island was quiet and sleepy, but it did nothing to cool his temper. He heard the rustle of palm trees and the incessant chirping of birds. Inez Key looked idyllic, but that was an illusion. Who knew such a small piece of land would cause him so much grief?

He looked over his shoulder and glared at the black roof of the main house. It may have been a dream home for some, but an image of the antebellum mansion had been in his nightmares since his childhood. He didn't see the gracious beauty but instead the cold emptiness. It was better suited as a museum than a family home. If he could, he would burn it down.

He would destroy the whole island if he had the chance, Sebastian thought grimly. He wanted to erase this particular ocean view. Get rid of the briny scent that still triggered bad memories. Wipe away the sunset that had been the backdrop of the night he had lost his innocent childhood.

No, he would keep the sunsets, Sebastian decided as he glanced at the cloudless sky. For the past month he had associated Ashley with sunsets. The orange-and-pink streaks were no longer ominous but instead held promise. He remembered every detail of the night Ashley had sat next to him on the veranda as they had watched the sun set.

Her warmth and soft femininity had cast a spell on him. He'd had trouble following their desultory conversation; Sebastian knew Ashley had been nervous that evening. It was as if she had known they would wind up in bed together. He had felt as if he could hear her heart pound against her ribs as a flush had crept into her cheeks.

Excitement had coiled around his chest when the stars blanketed the night sky. The thick and heavy air between them had crackled. She had teased his senses and a dangerous thrill had zipped through his veins.

Wild sensations had sparked inside him, pressing just under his skin when he had kissed her. That moment had been magical. Sebastian had meant to gently explore her lips, but the passion between them had exploded into something hot and urgent.

He'd keep the sunset, Sebastian decided. And the island, too. It was, after all, where he had first met Ashley. He didn't want to erase those moments he had shared with her, so the house must stay as well. It wouldn't be that great a hardship. Since he had stayed in the mansion with Ashley, Inez Key no longer had power over him.

He walked swiftly along the beach, following a bend that led to a cove. Sebastian paused and looked around, wondering where Ashley would hide. It would be somewhere that made her feel safe and protected. That could be anywhere on this small island. He had heard so many stories about Inez Key. As a kid who was raised on the dangerous streets, he had thought they were fairy tales.

His heart clenched when he saw Ashley curled in a tight ball next to a large piece of driftwood. Her damp jeans were caked with sand and she was almost dwarfed in her sweatshirt. Her hair was pulled up into a messy ponytail, but what he noticed the most was her tear-streaked face.

The anger slowly weakened as he stared at her. Ashley was suffering and he was to blame. When he first started this journey, he wanted to take away her safe little world. He got what he wanted and now he felt like a monster.

Sebastian had to fix this and get Ashley back. He needed her. Somehow he had been aware of it from the moment they met. He always knew this woman would be his redemption and his downfall. She would tame him and at the same time drive him wild.

He knew the moment Ashley saw him. Her body went rigid and she jumped up. Even from a distance, he could see Ashley was considering her options to pounce or make a run for it.

She wouldn't get far, he decided. He was ready to chase her, the thrill of the hunt in his blood. Ashley must have known that hiding was futile. Her shoulders sagged in defeat but she held her ground.

"What are you doing here?" she asked as she looked around the cove. "I didn't hear your speedboat."

"Which is why I took a different boat," he said as he walked toward her. He had known the only way he would find her was using the element of surprise. "Don't worry. I dismissed the security, so you don't have to hide."

Her eyes narrowed with suspicion and that annoyed him. Did she really think he'd lie about that? About everything? Did she think he lied with such fluency that he was incapable of speaking the truth?

"How'd you know I would be here?" she asked. "Did your security guards call you?"

"No, you managed to get past them. But then, you know all of the hiding places. It had been a lucky guess," he said as he stood in front of her. He wanted to grab her arms and shake her for making him worry. For making him chase her from country to country. And yet, he wanted to hold her close and not let her go.

"And it just happened to be your first guess?" Ashley clenched her jaw. "Am I that predictable?"

"It wasn't my first guess. I hunted down Salazar." He shoved his fists in the pockets of his hoodie. "He enjoyed that."

If he had hoped Ashley would show a hint of discomfort or remorse, he would have been greatly disappointed. "Good," she taunted. "Why should I be the only one embarrassed?"

"I'm very territorial and you know that," His low voice held an edge. "That's why you went off with him. It was a bad move."

"Is that what you think?" She raised her eyebrows with disbelief. "I don't base every decision on you. I had to get out of there and I took the first flight I could find. Salazar offered. Normally I would keep my distance from someone like him, but I was desperate."

"How desperate?" Sebastian asked. Ashley wasn't the kind of woman who would sleep with any interested man, but he knew how she responded when she was desperate and cornered. "How did you repay him for the favor?"

"What are you suggesting?" she snapped. "Do you think that I would sleep with him? Of course you do. After all, I'm sleeping with you for a chance to stay on this island."

"I don't think you had sex with Salazar," Sebastian said. Ashley was wild and sexy with him and *only* him. He had seen how she recoiled from Salazar's touch. She may have played on Salazar's twisted desires to get a ride home, but Ashley wouldn't touch another man. "I do, however, believe you went with him to hurt me."

She covered her face with her hands. "You're right. I did. I'm ashamed of what I did. I swore I would never act that way, and what happened? I allowed my emotions to take over. Oh, God. I'm just like her."

Her? Sebastian frowned. Who was Ashley comparing herself to?

"It doesn't matter how much I tried to…" She took a deep breath and lowered her hands. She squared back her shoulders and struggled to meet his gaze. "I'm sorry, Sebastian. I felt I had to leave but I didn't need to go with Salazar. There were other options. Better options. I can tell myself that I was desperate to get back here, but the truth is I wanted to swing back at you."

She'd succeeded. It was as if Ashley knew exactly where to strike. He must have lowered his guard or revealed how he felt when they were in bed. He was addicted to Ashley. He couldn't stop thinking about her, couldn't refrain from touching her. She was his weakness and she exploited it. Just as he knew Inez Key was her weak spot.

"Why is this place so important to you?" he asked. "Why are you willing to fight for just a piece of it?" He watched as she swallowed roughly. For a moment he didn't think she would answer.

"It's where I grew up," she said unevenly, as if she had to pull out the words. "It was a special place for me and my mother."

"That's it?" He sensed there was more. This island had a pull on Ashley that she couldn't break. What would cause that?

"No, it's more than that," she admitted. "Whenever the tabloids found out about my dad, my mom would bring me here. There was no TV, no internet and no paparazzi. We could stay here and heal."

"You're lucky you had this place," he said harshly. "I would have killed for this island when I was a child."

"I'm not so sure." She held her arms close to her body. "Sometimes I felt like my mom used this place to hide from reality. The lack of distractions should have given her some clarity. Instead, it became a cocoon that blocked out all the facts. It gave my dad a chance to hide the worst of his sins. He would beg for forgiveness, swear it was all lies, and we would head back to the mainland until the cycle started all over again."

Inez Key wasn't quite the haven he thought it was for Ashley. It was connected to good memories and bad. It was part of her childhood and the loss of her innocence.

"And there is no need to escort me off the premises.

I'm going." Ashley announced. She bent down to brush the sand off her jeans.

"You'll leave with me and return to Miami."

"Our deal is off," she said as she straightened and dusted off her hands. "From the moment you broke your promise."

"Which one?" he muttered.

She narrowed her eyes. "I'm confused. What are you saying?"

"About last night…" He took a deep breath. This was going to be difficult but it couldn't be ignored. "We didn't use protection."

Ashley went pale as she stared at him. She didn't say a word. He wasn't sure how she was going to handle the news. From the way she interacted with the young islanders, he knew she liked children. Sebastian could easily imagine that she would be a fierce and protective mother. But that didn't mean she liked the idea of having *his* children.

"I apologize," Sebastian said as he raked his hand through his hair. "I don't know what happened. I always remember to use protection."

His claim seemed to wake her up. "Of course you do," she said in a withering tone.

"I'm serious." He watched her stalk past him. "I don't take any unnecessary risks."

"I'm sure you believe that," she said over her shoulder.

"But you don't." He had been careful about protection every time. It hadn't been easy. He almost forgot on more than one occasion, so caught up in the moment that nothing else seemed to matter. It had never been like that with any other woman.

But why didn't she take his word for it? Why was she that determined to see the worst in him? "It doesn't matter what you believe," he decided. "It was my responsibility and I failed you."

Ashley turned around. "Sebastian, I don't need you to take care of me. I can take care of myself. I've been doing that since I can remember."

"There's no chance of you being on the Pill?" he asked hopefully.

Ashley glared at him. "What do you think? You were my first." Her voice rose with every word. "I never had a need until I met you and I wasn't planning a repeat performance."

"We've been together for weeks and you still haven't considered protecting yourself from pregnancy. Why is that? You know, there are a lot of women who live well because they had a rich man's baby." He didn't think Ashley was one of those women, but he also knew his judgment was impaired when she was around.

Ashley rubbed her hands over her face and blew out an exasperated puff of air. "I have no interest in getting pregnant, no interest in having your baby, and I no longer have any interest in this conversation."

He ignored the sting from her words. "You have to admit that this is a concern." He needed to be more careful next time. He needed her to trust him so that there *would* be a next time.

She looked away and stared at the water. As if seeing the ocean would calm her and give her a sense of peace. "Is this how you respond whenever you have a pregnancy scare?" she asked.

He clenched his teeth. "I've never had one because I always use protection."

She pressed her lips together. "I find it hard to believe that a man with your—" she paused "—legendary sex life has not had any paternity suits, payoffs or baby drama."

"Believe it," he said in a growl.

"Every time I think I'm wrong about you, I am slapped with the truth. You remind me a lot of my father. He was something of a playboy." Her lip curled in a sneer when she said the word. "He was supposed to be a tennis legend, but he's known more for his sexual escapades and paternity suits."

"I am not a playboy," he insisted. He hated the word. It diminished everything that he had achieved. "And I'm nothing like your father."

"Right. Right." She raised her hand to stop him. "Because you're smarter. You use protection. Sometimes."

"Ashley, I give you my word." He grabbed her arm and held her still, but she looked the other way. "If you become pregnant, I will take care of you and the baby."

She whipped her head around and stared at him. "You would? Why?"

He was offended by her surprise. "You and the child would be my responsibility."

She tilted her head as she studied him with open suspicion. "What do you mean by taking care?"

"I would take care of you financially and I would be involved in the child's life." He would want a lot more, but he would wait to discuss it if there was a child. There was no reason to tell Ashley every sacrifice he would make for his family.

"Really?" She pulled away from his grasp. "You wouldn't ask for a termination or take legal action against me and swear I'm lying about the paternity?"

"What kind of man do you think I am? No, don't answer that." He was already feeling volatile and he knew he wasn't going to like what Ashley had to say.

"It's what my father did," she said with disgust. "It's what most men do."

"You don't know much about men. Or me." Sebastian took a step forward until they were almost touching. He noticed Ashley didn't back down. Most people would. "I take care of my family. That would include you and the baby."

She frowned and studied his face. "This doesn't make any sense."

"Let me make it clear to you," he said through gritted teeth. "If you are pregnant with my child, I will give him my last name. I will let everyone know that he is mine and that I take care of what is mine. I will protect and provide for him."

She stared at him as if in a daze.

"And if I need to marry his mother," he forced the words out, "I will do so."

Her mouth dropped open. "Are you serious?"

"But don't take that as a marriage proposal," he warned. "The only reason I would marry any woman is if she was carrying my child."

CHAPTER EIGHT

"COME ON, ASHLEY, we'll discuss this later. We need to leave," Sebastian said as he stuffed his hands in his hoodie pocket. He was never comfortable with the topic of marriage. The idea of sacrificing his freedom usually made him break into a cold sweat. Right now, he felt the hope and longing swirl inside him as he imagined Ashley's belly swollen with his child.

"Already?" she said with a sigh.

He heard the longing in her voice and hated how it affected him. Sebastian wanted to make her happy. He wanted to give her everything she wanted and be the reason there was a smile on her face. He glanced at his watch. "You can show me around the island before we leave."

Ashley's eyes lit up, but she gave him a suspicious look. "Really?" she asked uncertainly. As if she knew he was trying to make up for the argument they'd just had.

"Show me everything about Inez Key," he said. He knew a lot about this island, but he wanted to see it through her eyes.

Ashley grabbed his hand. "First, I'll show where the best place is to scuba dive. Oh, and surf. Did I tell you about the time I got stung by an eagle ray? It was an extremely painful experience, but not as much as when I broke my ankle when I fell from climbing a palm tree. I'll have to show you which ones are best to climb."

"I can't wait," Sebastian said with a small smile. He was curious to know what Ashley was like as a child and wanted to hear every story and anecdote.

They had explored the island for an hour, hand in hand, as Ashley pointed out her favorite spots. Some were connected to happy memories while others were breathtaking views.

"Do you know how the island got the name Inez Key?" Sebastian asked as he walked beside Ashley.

"It's called a key because it's a small island on coral," she explained.

"And Inez?"

"I assume the first settler on this island named it after a loved one." She stared at the main house as she slowed her pace. Her tour was almost done and then she would have to leave Inez Key.

"Assume?" he asked sharply.

"Okay, I'm not an expert on everything about this island. You should ask Clea. Her family has been on this island for generations," Ashley said as her smile dipped. Once she thought her descendants would live here for generations. She had imagined having a big family and the island being their safe haven. "Now that you mention it, I'm surprised my father didn't change the name. Make it Jones Key or something like that. Are you going to change the name?"

"Never."

His gruff response surprised her. "Why not? The name doesn't have any meaning to you."

Sebastian's hand flexed against hers. "How long have you lived here?" he asked.

"This wasn't our primary residence," she replied as she focused her attention on the main house. "I spent my summers on this island. My mother brought me here when she needed a getaway."

"So it wasn't used very often," he murmured. "It was almost forgotten."

"I'm sure it wasn't always like that. It's been in my family's care since before I was born. My father got it—"

"Got it?"

Ashley bit her tongue. Funny how he caught her choice of words. The man noticed everything. She had to be more careful. "My father's story about this island changed constantly," she admitted.

"What did you hear?" he asked as he slipped his hand away from hers.

She felt the tension emanating from Sebastian and hesitated. She didn't like revealing her family history. It offered people a chance to question her heritage and judge her. "It's difficult to extract the truth from the legend. Some say my father won it in a poker game. Others suggested it was a gift from a woman. I once heard a politician bought it for him in exchange for silence."

"What do you think happened?"

I think he stole it. She didn't know how her father had got the island, but she knew what kind of man he was. He cheated on and off the tennis court, but that wasn't her only clue. She remembered the sly look in his eyes when he spoke of Inez Key. She knew something bad happened and she had been too hesitant to dig deeper.

Ashley forced herself to give a casual shrug as she marched to the main house. "It's hard to say."

"I'm sure you have a theory." Sebastian watched her carefully.

"Not really," she said in a rush as they stood by the columns in the back of the main house. "Well, that's it of Inez Key."

"Don't you have more stories to tell?"

Ashley returned his smile. She had talked endlessly about her childhood adventures on Inez Key, but Sebastian hadn't seemed bored. He had been genuinely interested. "That's for another day," she promised.

"Thank you for sharing your stories," he said gently. "And for showing me your island."

She suddenly felt shy, as if she had shared a secret part of her. Ashley felt the warmth rush through her. "What's your favorite part of Inez Key?"

"The cove," he said. "It's the perfect hideout. No wonder the sea turtles nest there."

Ashley frowned. She didn't remember telling him about the nests that are laid during springtime. "How did you know we have sea turtles?"

Sebastian paused. "Uh, I think Clea said something about it."

"We usually get the loggerhead turtle to nest on our

island. Two months later, all of these hatchlings find their way to the water. It's an amazing sight."

"I'm sure it is," he murmured.

"I think the sea turtles pick this place because there aren't that many predators. The island is a good hideaway for people, too. The paparazzi never bothers us." Not even when her father was caught up in one scandal after another. She didn't know if it was because it was hard to find the remote island or because no journalist found it worthwhile to follow the betrayed mother and child.

Sebastian saw the shadows in her eyes. Was she recalling a bad memory from her childhood or was she reluctant to leave. "It's time to go, *mi vida*."

Ashley bit her lip. "Can't we stay just for the night?"

"Impossible." He didn't want Ashley to stay any longer. It was Cruz property now and the last thing he needed was the previous owner hanging around causing trouble. "I need to be at my mother's tomorrow morning."

"I'm sure she didn't extend the invitation to me," she said. "I can stay here until you return."

Sebastian hated that idea. He didn't want to spend another night away from Ashley. He hadn't been able to sleep and he ached all night to have her in his arms. The idea of finding a replacement hadn't even occurred to him. He only wanted Ashley.

"You forget our agreement," he said silkily. "You are supposed to be with me every day for a month. You missed a few days when you skipped out on me in Jamaica. That's going to cost you."

"Cost me?" Her face paled as she looked around her beloved Inez Key. "What do you mean?"

"You have not been with me for a consecutive thirty days," he explained. He smiled as he realized this gave him the chance to keep Ashley at his side for a little bit longer. "I'm adding those missing days at the end of your month."

Her lips parted in surprise. "That was not agreed upon."

He didn't care. He had torn through Miami looking for this woman and he wasn't ready to give her up. "Would you rather we start over and make this day one?"

Something hot and wild flared in her eyes. Ashley dipped her head as she dug her foot in the sand. "I thought you'd be bored staying with one woman for a month."

Sebastian frowned. That had been true, but not with Ashley. Now he was trying to find ways to keep her in his bed.

"Wait a second." Ashley lifted her head and stared at him with something close to horror. "Does this mean I'm meeting your mother? No. No way."

"I don't have much of a choice. Anyway, she's expecting you."

Ashley closed her eyes and slowly shook her head. "Do you usually introduce your mistress to your mother?" she asked huskily.

"I've never had a mistress," he admitted.

Ashley opened her eyes and stared at him.

Sebastian scowled. He hadn't planned to tell her that,

but for some reason it was suddenly important for her to understand that he wasn't that kind of man. Yet now he felt exposed under her gaze. As if he'd revealed too much of himself. "Don't think that makes you special."

Ashley glared at him. "Why should I? You had pushed me in a corner so efficiently. It was only natural to assume you blackmailed women in your bed on a regular basis."

He stepped closer. "You wanted to be in my bed," he declared. "I only had to give you an extra incentive."

She gave a haughty tilt to her chin. "Think that if it makes you feel better."

He curled a finger under her chin and brushed his thumb against her wide pink mouth. "You will need to curb your tongue before you meet my family," he warned her softly.

She tried to nip his thumb with her teeth, but he had anticipated that response. He removed his hand before she could catch him.

"I can't make any promises," she said and paused. "Did you say I'm meeting your family? I thought it was just your mother."

"My sisters will be there. That means their husbands, fiancés and children will also be around."

"Why? Is there a special occasion?"

"No, my family has these get-togethers all the time." And he worked hard to be there for his family. He didn't just write a check for his relatives—he was present for every important moment of their lives.

"Is there anything I should know about your family?" she asked.

"Do not introduce yourself as my mistress," he ordered.

She clucked her tongue. "Do you think I wear that label as a badge of honor?"

"You made it clear in Jamaica that you are my woman." He reached for her hand and laced his fingers with hers. "I didn't have to make a claim. You wore that status with pride."

"That was before you introduced me as your mistress," she said as the anger tightened her soft features. "I thought we actually made a good team until you warned off Salazar. Then you had to mark your territory. So how am I supposed to define this relationship?"

He was not going to introduce Ashley as his lover or girlfriend. That gave her privileges she didn't deserve. The reason he made Ashley his mistress was to knock down the status she never worked hard to earn. "You won't need to."

"Are you serious?" She tugged at his hand but he didn't let go. "Didn't you tell me you had sisters?"

"Yes, four of them."

"And how often have you brought a woman home to meet the family?" she asked brightly.

He exhaled sharply. "I haven't."

"You are in for an inquisition." Ashley smiled broadly as she imagined the treatment he would receive.

Or she was dreaming up ways to make his life miserable. He could send Ashley back to his penthouse apartment while he went to visit his family, but he didn't like that idea. He wanted Ashley there with him, but it was a risk. "Cause any trouble and you will regret it."

She flattened her hand against her chest. "Me? I won't have to say a word. I'll just cling to your arm and bat my lashes like a good little mistress."

"Ashley," he warned.

"At least tell me why we need to visit your family. Isn't your mother recuperating?"

He gave her an assessing glance. "How do you know about that?"

"What? Was it a secret? You said something about it at the opening of your club. I've often heard you talk to your mother on the phone."

Sebastian's eyes narrowed. "I didn't realize you knew Spanish." How much had she heard in his conversations? Did she also catch the endearments he whispered when they were in bed? He had to be more careful.

"I'm not fluent," she said. "I don't know anything about your mother's condition."

"She's recovering from heart surgery," he explained. "There had been a point when we didn't think she was going to make it. My mother made a dying request and we called the priest."

Ashley squeezed his hand in silent sympathy. "I won't do anything to upset her. I promise."

"Thank you." Sebastian realized how he was gripping her hand as if it was a lifeline. He reluctantly let go. "I don't want you to discuss our relationship with anyone in my family. Don't mention Inez Key. In fact, don't give any personal information."

"Should I pick an assumed name?" she asked wryly.

"Ashley Jones should be fine." It was a common name. His family wouldn't make the connection.

"Okay," she said with a shrug. "If that's what you want."

Her quick agreement made him suspicious. "What are you up to?"

"Nothing. I'll just keep the conversation all about you." She rubbed her hands with exaggerated glee. "I can't wait to learn all your secrets."

Dread seized his lungs until he remembered that there was an unspoken agreement with his family on some topics that were forbidden to discuss. "Good luck with that," he said with icy calm. "I don't have any."

Ashley made a face. "Everyone has secrets."

"You don't anymore," he said. "I uncovered them all when I took you to bed."

"You are so hung up on being my first," she muttered. Ashley looked flustered and shy. "If I knew that my virginity would have been so important to you…"

Sebastian stepped in front of her, blocking her from turning away. "What would you have done?" he asked. She had not been above using her virginity with Raymond Casillas to get what she wanted. "Keep away from me until I begged? Waited for a wedding ring on your finger?"

"No!" she said, staring at him with wide eyes. "I would have told you."

Would it have been that simple? Could their first night have been about two people giving in to a fiery attraction? "Why didn't you?"

"I didn't want you to know how inexperienced I was," she confessed as a ruddy color streaked her high cheekbones. "It would have given you the upper hand."

He always had the advantage even with the most experienced women. Although there had been some nights with Ashley when he wasn't sure who was seducing whom. She had gradually begun to realize the depths of his excitement when she made the first move. She was beginning to tap into the sexual power she held over him. He should hide his responses, or at least take over when she became too daring, but he didn't want to.

"You had nothing to worry about, *mi vida*. You're a very sensual woman." He noticed how his compliment horrified her. "I'm surprised you abstained for as long as you did. Why did you wait?"

"Lack of opportunity?" she hazarded a guess.

She was not telling him the truth. Not the whole truth. "That's not it at all," he said gently. "Men would subject themselves to Herculean tasks if it meant a chance for one night with you."

"Every man but you," she muttered. "You just had to snap your fingers and I was there."

"Why did you wait?" he repeated. What he really wanted to ask was, *Why did you choose me?*

"If you saw the house I was raised in you would understand." She crossed her arms and looked at the ocean, unable to meet his eyes. "My mother was a mistress. A sexual plaything for my father. My father was a womanizer. He was worse than his friends. The things I saw…heard. I didn't want to be a part of that."

Sebastian felt a sharp arrow of guilt. Shame. He was beginning to think he had made a mistake when he'd claimed Ashley as his mistress. He thought she didn't like the drop in status. Instead, he had made her the one thing she swore she would never be.

"And yet you slept with me." It didn't add up. Did she sleep with him so she could stop Raymond Casillas from calling in her debt? "According to you, I'm just like your father."

"I thought you were," she said quietly before she walked away. "I'm not so sure anymore."

The next evening, Ashley was on a luxurious patio that overlooked a private beach as she watched the sunset with Sebastian's mother. A group of children were playing in the sand. Music drifted from the open windows of the Cruz mansion and Ashley heard Sebastian's sisters bicker while they prepared the dinner table.

"Why is this the first I've heard of you?" Patricia Cruz asked as she intently studied Ashley.

Ashley hid her smile. She had a feeling that Sebastian took from his mother's side in temperament. "I don't know what to tell you, Mrs. Cruz. Perhaps you should ask Sebastian."

She gave a throaty chuckle. "He's not very forthcoming."

Neither was his mother. The older woman wasn't a tiny and weathered woman who favored housedresses and heavy shawls. This woman was tall and regal. Her elegant gray shift dress highlighted her short silver hair and tanned skin.

Patricia Esteban Cruz was polite but wary. She had expected Sebastian's family and home to be just as guarded. When Ashley had seen the iron gates open to the Cruz's beachfront mansion, panic had curled around her chest. She had looked out the window and saw a forest of palm trees flanking the long driveway.

Ashley had tried not to gasp when she spotted the villa at the end of the winding lane. The home was unlike anything she had seen. She had expected the Cruz mansion to be a dramatic and modern house. A fortress. But this was gracious and traditional with its terra-cotta rooftops and soft white exterior. Ashley was used to high society but this was another level. It was a reminder of Sebastian's power and influence.

"His sisters, however, are very warm and open," Ashley said. They had easily welcomed her. Sebastian's siblings were boisterous and inquisitive, but they had made Ashley feel as if she belonged.

And they had no reservations talking about Sebastian. At first it had been a trickle of information and it quickly became a flood of memories. The anecdotes and stories all described Sebastian as curious, volatile and too smart for his own good. He had been a lot of trouble, but everyone spoke about him with pride, love and exasperation.

"Yes, they didn't have as hard of a time as Sebastian," she said with a heavy sigh. "When my husband died, Sebastian became the head of the family. He was only a boy. Not even fifteen."

There was a fine tremor in the woman's fingers and Ashley noticed the gray pallor underneath the woman's skin. It was clear Patricia was still fragile from her surgery. "Sebastian doesn't talk about that time in his life. Or his father."

"He lives with the constant reminder," the older woman said. "He looks just like his father. My husband was very much a traditional man. Proud and artistic."

"Your husband was an artist?" Ashley asked.

She nodded. "He was a painter. Watercolors. He wasn't famous, but he was very respected in the art world. Some of his landscapes can be found here in my home." Patricia's eyes grew sad. "He stopped painting when we moved to the ghetto. He was working two jobs and feeding a growing family."

This was why Sebastian scoffed at the way she made a living. She may repair and maintain Inez Key, but she never had to do hard labor. She didn't know the strain of having a family depend on her.

"Which of your children inherited your husband's artistic talent?" From what she could tell, all of the Cruz daughters were brilliant, successful and creative.

"Mmm, that would be Sebastian."

"Really?" Sebastian thrived in the cutthroat business world. She hadn't seen any indication that he had an artistic side.

"You should have seen the work he did at school," Patricia said with a hint of pride. "His teachers encouraged him to find classes outside of school. If only we had the money. But Sebastian told he me didn't have the inclination to pursue it."

Ashley imagined Sebastian saying that with a dismissive wave of his hand. But she wondered if Sebastian didn't choose the arts because he had to be sensible. He would have known it would have been a financial strain for the family and he acted disinterested to protect his mother's feelings.

"Well, if there's one thing I've noticed about Sebastian," Ashley said brightly, "he can do anything he puts his mind to. If he had wanted to be an artist, he would have been."

"And what is it that you do, Ashley?" Sebastian's mother asked. "You're twenty-three? I'm sure you have found your passion by now."

Ashley knew it was another attempt to learn about her past. She wasn't willing to share, and not just because of Sebastian's request. It was unlikely that she would meet Patricia Esteban Cruz again, but she didn't want to be judged by her parentage.

"I'm still trying to figure that out," Ashley carefully replied. "What did you want to be when you were twenty-three?"

"Home." Patricia had a faraway look in her eyes. "I wanted to be home, safe and sound with my babies while my husband was happily painting pictures of sunsets and nighthawks."

Nighthawks? Ashley frowned. Those birds were indigenous to the keys. She hadn't realized they were up here on the mainland.

Ashley turned sharply when she heard the piercing squeal of a child's laughter. She saw Sebastian, sexy and casual in a T-shirt and jeans, at the edge of the beach. The water lapped at his bare feet as he held one of his nephews in his strong hands.

"More, Tio Sebastian! More!" the little boy shrieked as Sebastian tossed him high in the air before catching him. One of his nieces clung to Sebastian's legs with her thumb firmly planted in her mouth. Ashley noticed the toddler had attached herself to her tio Sebastian the moment they had arrived.

"Ah, my grandchildren are precious to me, but they wear me out," Patricia confessed as she watched the trio on the beach. "Sebastian is so patient with them. Gives each of his nieces and nephews extra attention. If only he was so patient with his sisters."

"He's very good with children." She remembered how gentle he had been with Clea's granddaughters on Inez Key. Ashley had been concerned Sebastian would be like most of her paying guests who didn't want to hear or see children on the island. She recalled how he had found them playing on the beach one day and when he had approached them, Ashley's first thought had been to protect them. Ashley thought the girls would have been scared or intimidated by Sebastian. But he had surprised her when he had crouched down in front of the curious children and got down to their level.

A smile tugged on Ashley's mouth as she remembered that hot and humid morning. The scene had been so incongruous with Sebastian's dark head next to Lizet and Matil, who wore silly hats to protect them from the sun. He had given the girls his full attention, speaking in a low voice as he praised their efforts in building a sand castle.

The children immediately adored him, with Lizet shyly offering her battered pink bucket while Matil danced excitedly around them. Ashley had quietly watched as Sebastian had played with the children.

She had been amazed by the gentleness and patience he had displayed.

"He would make a good father," Patricia declared.

Ashley wanted to reject that idea. Sebastian was a playboy. A good father would be sweet and tender. A family man. He wouldn't be someone like her father who would destroy a family in his pursuit to have sex with many women.

But Sebastian wasn't like Donald Jones, Ashley realized with a start. Sebastian cared about his family. Family was his haven, not his burden. He honored his commitments and was willing to put his family's needs before his. And he would protect his loved ones instead of overpowering them.

Ashley knew she would be included if she was carrying his baby. She closed her eyes and imagined Sebastian holding her close as his fingers splayed against her swollen stomach. His touch would be gentle and possessive. He would not allow anything to happen to them as a family. As a couple.

"Do you think differently?" Patricia asked, jarring Ashley from her musings. "Do you think Sebastian would make a bad father?"

"He would be the father any child would hope for," Ashley said slowly as she thought about how Sebastian embodied everything she hoped for in a man, a husband, and yet he was also everything she feared. "But I don't think he has the inclination to become one."

"That's what I'm worried about. Sebastian had to look after his sisters at such a young age. He may not want to do it again. But that man should have a wife. Children of his own."

"Carry on the Cruz name?" Ashley added as she absently rubbed her flat stomach. She wanted Sebastian's child. More than one. She wanted to create a large family filled with sons and daughters that had the same dark hair, stubbornness and strength as their father. Most of all, she wanted to see those children bring out Sebastian's fierce paternal side.

"Exactly." Patricia smacked her armrest with her hand like a judge would bang a gavel. "He should marry."

Don't look at me. Ashley gritted her teeth before the words tumbled off her tongue. Men didn't marry their mistresses. She had it on good authority. Her mother had tried every trick for twenty years to make Donald her husband.

Donald and Linda may have shared a past and a child, but they never shared a family name. Donald had given his surname to Ashley, but she had never understood why. Why had she been considered good enough for the Jones name and not her mother?

But Sebastian was different, Ashley thought as she watched him set down his nephew and hoist his small niece into his arms. He would marry her if she was carrying his child. She longed for a traditional family but not like this. If she was pregnant with his baby, she would have some tough decisions to make. She had been tolerated in her father's home, part of a package deal. Ashley wasn't going to go through that again.

* * *

Later that night, Sebastian stepped out of the bathroom and into the guest bedroom. The steam from his shower curled around him as he slung a towel low around his waist. His heart beat against his ribs as he anticipated having Ashley all to himself.

He stopped in the middle of the room when he noticed Ashley wasn't in the large bed waiting for him. She wasn't in the sitting area or at the desk. Sebastian turned and saw Ashley standing at the long open window, the gauzy curtains billowing against her.

Desire slammed through him as he noticed how the silk slip skimmed against her gentle curves. The dark pink accentuated her sun-kissed skin and the short hem barely reached her thighs. He was tempted to pull the delicate shoulder straps until they broke and watch the silk tumble to the floor.

It took him a moment to notice that Ashley was waving at someone outside. "Who are you waving to?" he asked gruffly. As much as he enjoyed the sight, he was prepared to cloak her with something heavy. He should be the only one who saw her like this.

"Your sister Ana Sofia and her husband," she responded without looking at him. "Apparently, they take a moonlight stroll along the beach every night."

"I'm sure that's real romantic when it's pouring down rain." He refused to hear the catch in her throat. "You and Ana Sofia were thick as thieves tonight."

She turned away from the window and he saw her smile. "She wanted to tell me all of the mean things you did to her while you were growing up. I have to say, none of it surprised me."

"I had to be strict with her," he said as he approached her. "I'm her big brother and our father had died."

She nodded. "I understand, but you're lucky you had your sisters."

"It didn't feel so lucky," he muttered.

"Well, I was an only child. I would have loved a sister or two."

He noticed Ashley had watched how his family interacted with a mix of amusement and bewilderment. "They were in full force today. You didn't find them overwhelming?"

"It took some time to get used to it," she admitted. "Your sisters got a little vocal at the dinner table."

"That?" He rested his hand against the wall and he leaned into her. "That was nothing."

She gave him a look of disbelief. "You were arguing about a vase that broke almost twenty years ago."

"I was blamed for that because I was supposed to be looking after my sisters." He hadn't been surprised that Ashley didn't side with him during the argument. Did she still see him as the opposition? The enemy? "Ana Sofia was the one who actually broke it."

"Twenty years ago," she reminded him. "You can certainly hold a grudge."

"You have no idea." He gritted his teeth and took a step back. Sebastian wasn't going to reveal just how much a grudge motivated him. Dominated his thoughts. "I'm sure this happened in your house, too. Who were you able to blame when you broke something? The family dog?"

"It never happened, but I don't think my parents would have noticed. Quite a few breakables were thrown against the wall during an argument in my house," she said matter-of-factly. "And I can't count how much damage occurred during one of my father's famous house parties."

Was this why Ashley didn't drink or party? Why she didn't enjoy dancing and preferred her solitude? He wouldn't blame her. Ashley's home life was more of a war zone than a wonderland. "How did you escape? Did you spend a lot of time at a friend's house?"

"Not really. Once their parents found out that I was a mistress's love child I wasn't invited over. Something about being a bad influence." She grimaced as if she had tasted something unpleasant. "Love child. It sounds like I was born out of love, but I wasn't. I hate that label."

And she hated the label of mistress. He didn't know that it would hurt her so much. He didn't know she had been an outcast because of the stigma. He had made a power play without considering Ashley's past. But how could he fix it now?

Ashley raked her hand over her hair and rolled back her shoulders. Sebastian had seen that movement before. He knew this was a sign that she was finished with the conversation.

"I've been meaning to ask," she said as she walked away. "Did your father paint this watercolor?"

His gaze flew to the framed picture that hung on the wall. He'd forgotten about the picture of the sunset. "Yes."

"It's very good," she said as she walked to the bed-side table and gave the picture a closer look. "It reminds me a lot of the sunsets I see on Inez Key. It kind of makes me homesick."

The longing in her quiet tone scored at him. He wasn't going to fall for this guilt trip. He had to be strict with Ashley or she would soon discover that he was willing to give her almost anything she wanted.

"Is this another attempt to go back to the island?" he asked as he followed her.

She jerked her head in surprise and turned to face him. "No. I'm a mistress for a month and I have to be at your beck and call for a little over two weeks. I can wait."

The pang of guilt intensified. He should honor his word and allow her to become the caretaker for Inez Key. But he didn't want her on the island. She didn't belong there. Ashley Jones belonged in his bed and at his side.

"What if we renegotiated?" he asked.

Ashley frowned and she studied his expression, as if trying to determine whether he was reneging. "What are you talking about?"

"The time frame remains the same but we drop the mistress part," he suggested as he reached for her. "Forget the rules I set in place."

She pressed her hand against his bare chest. Her fingers curled in the damp mat of his dark hair. "What's the catch?"

"No catch," he said as he moved closer.

"Is this renegotiation because you don't want your mistress in your family home," she asked, "or because you can't tolerate the idea that your mistress might be having your baby?"

"You know, I should have walked away when you broke your promise," he said. "You were supposed to be available to me at all times, but you went off with Salazar for a few days."

Ashley gave an exasperated sigh. "You make that sound much more scandalous that it was. And may I remind you that you broke both of my rules?"

"Do you want to drop the mistress label or not?" he asked roughly as he gathered her tightly until her body was flush with his.

She swiped her tongue along her bottom lip. "What would I be known as instead?" she whispered.

"Mine."

He saw the flare of heat in her dark eyes. She dipped her head and looked away. "I'm serious."

"As Ashley." *My Ashley. My woman. Mi vida. Mine.* And the next man who tried to take her away from him would deeply regret it.

Ashley frowned and lifted her head to meet his gaze. "Do you still expect total obedience?"

"If it hasn't happened yet, it's not going to," he said as he pressed his mouth against the fluttering pulse point at the base of her throat. He liked how trusting and wild she was in his arms. That was all he needed.

"I can make my own decisions on which events to attend with you?" Ashley asked, her breath hitching as he shoved the delicate strap down her shoulder. "And what I'm going to wear?"

Sebastian cupped her breast with his large hand. He

felt her tight nipple against his palm. "Yes," he said almost in a daze.

"And tonight I could get my own bedroom?"

He stilled as something close to fear forked through him. "No," he said with a growl. He should have known that if he gave her an inch, she'd take a mile. The only hold he had left on Ashley was the sexual chemistry they shared. She couldn't hide her emotions, her needs, when they were in bed. He wasn't going to allow any distance between them.

"Why not?" she teased. "Is it really that important to you? I—"

"You are not kicking me out of your bed again. You don't want sex tonight? Fine," he snapped. "But we're sharing the same bed. Always."

"It's a deal," she said with a seductive smile. "And Sebastian?"

"What?" His tone was harsh as the relief poured through him.

"I want you tonight," she said as she reached for the towel wrapped around his waist. "All night and every night."

"I've noticed," he drawled as his heart pounded in his ears. Sebastian lifted Ashley and she wrapped her legs around his waist. He had wondered when she was going to admit that she couldn't keep her hands off him. He knew she wouldn't have made the confession as a mistress.

This impetuous renegotiation was going to give him everything he wanted.

CHAPTER NINE

THE ELEGANT SOUTH BEACH restaurant offered a spectacular view and an award-winning menu, but Sebastian barely noticed. He didn't care that he had a mountain of work waiting for him at the office or that some of the most powerful people in Miami were sitting nearby, hoping to catch his eye. Nothing mattered except the exquisite brunette at his side.

Sebastian leaned back in his chair and smiled as he heard Ashley's earthy laugh. It made him tingle as if a spray of fireworks lit under his skin. Ashley's laugh was one of his most favorite sounds. It was right up there with her moan of pleasure and the way her breath hitched in her throat when he knew just how to touch her.

He watched Ashley as his friend Omar told her about one of their ill-conceived childhood antics. Omar embellished the story, making it sound as if he'd saved Sebastian from a gruesome death instead of the daily violence they had faced. His friend's wife shook her head as she listened to the story with a mix of horror and amusement.

Sebastian wished he could freeze this moment. It was rare for him to feel content. Satisfied. Hopeful. He didn't allow himself a lot of downtime. He couldn't remember the last time he'd spent the evening with his friends. Sebastian didn't feel the need to relax and have a drink. He was always pursuing the next challenge, creating the next strategy.

All that changed once he had Ashley at his side. His body tightened with lust as he studied her. She wore her hair piled high on her head. He was tempted to reach over, pull the pins and watch the heavy waves fall past her bare shoulders. He suspected she chose the style to tease him all evening.

Her dress was another matter. Short, strapless and scarlet, Ashley had worn it to please him. She knew how to showcase her curves and she was aware that his favorite color was red. The bold cleavage made him grit his teeth, but he was secretly touched that she dressed with him in mind.

He was glad she chose to be at his side tonight and every night. Not as his mistress, but as... As what? His lover? His girlfriend? Possibly the mother of his child? He was reluctant to give her that kind of power or accept her claim in his life. He wasn't sure what Ashley was, but she was important to him.

But their month was almost up. If she wasn't pregnant, he had to let her go. Unless he followed through and allowed her to become the caretaker of Inez Key. It wasn't an ideal choice since he wasn't going to live on the island. But he planned to visit frequently....

Ashley tilted her head back and laughed. "I can just

picture it," she said between gasps as she flattened her hands against her chest. "You two were trouble."

"Wait a second!" Crystal's eyes lit up as she pointed her finger at Ashley. "Now I know why you look familiar."

Sebastian saw Ashley stiffen. He wanted to silence Omar's wife. Protect Ashley. It was unfair for Ashley. She had lowered her guard only to be confronted with her family history.

"You are the daughter of that tennis legend," Crystal exclaimed.

"Yes, I am," Ashley confirmed quietly as she reached for her water glass. "How did you know?"

"Like I said, I am a news junkie," Crystal said proudly. "There was something about the way the light hit your face. You look exactly like your mother."

"Thank you," Ashley said. Was it only Sebastian who noticed the pain that flashed in her eyes? Linda Valdez had been a beautiful woman, but Ashley didn't like being compared to her mother.

"Who are you talking about?" Omar asked his wife.

"Ashley's father was Donald Jones. The tennis star," Crystal explained.

Sebastian admired Ashley's calm. He knew what she was thinking. That his friends were going to see her differently because she was a love child and her mother was a mistress. Because her parents died in a murder-suicide.

She would soon learn that his friends—his true friends—didn't judge. After surviving the ghetto and witnessing the darker side of humanity, nothing shocked them.

"Donald…Jones?" Omar repeated slowly and gave Sebastian a quick glance.

Damn. Sebastian's gut twisted with alarm. He'd forgotten that Omar knew how his past was intertwined with Donald Jones. Sebastian gave the slightest shake of his head and Omar immediately went quiet. He hoped Ashley didn't notice the silent exchange.

"Oh, I'm sure I have mascara streaming down my face," Ashley murmured as she pressed her fingertips underneath her eyes. She grabbed for her purse and stood up. "I'll have to fix my makeup."

Sebastian quietly rose from the table. He knew Ashley wanted to hide. Just for a moment so she could firmly fix the cool mask she displayed to the public. The one that made people think she lived a quiet and uneventful life on a private island.

"I'll come with you," Crystal offered as she scrambled out of her seat.

Ashley didn't say anything, but Sebastian noticed the tension in her polite smile. He wanted to intervene and protect her from the intrusive questions Crystal would undoubtedly ask. He couldn't. His guarded response would create more questions.

He reached for her and pressed his lips against her temple. He felt Ashley lean against him briefly before she stepped away. He wanted to block Crystal, but Ashley was experienced in facing this kind of attention with grace.

He sat down once the women left the table and immediately faced Omar's disapproving glare. "Donald

Jones?" his friend asked angrily. "It can't be a coincidence."

He wasn't going to insult his friend with a lie. "It's not."

Omar rubbed his forehead and exhaled sharply. "What have you done, Sebastian?"

He jutted out his chin. "I settled an old score. Karma was taking too long."

"I thought you put all this behind you," Omar said. He looked around to make sure no one could hear the conversation. "You've become richer and more powerful than Jones."

That didn't mean he'd won. "It doesn't erase what he did."

Omar shook his head. "I don't get it. Why now? Why, after all this time?"

There had been a time when Sebastian had been consumed by the injustice. It ate away at him, making him feel weak and empty. He had been an angry boy. He had been a kid who'd lost his innocence too soon and his childhood the moment he had been thrown into a cruel world. He wanted to get what was stolen from him and pushed himself every day to the brink of exhaustion to become rich and powerful.

He had suffered setbacks and bad luck, but by the time he had made his first million, Sebastian wasn't thinking about Donald Jones. His goal had been to protect his family from losing everything. They would never be at the mercy of the Donald Joneses of the world.

But then his mother had heart surgery, and everything changed. He realized he was still the angry little boy who couldn't allow the injustice to go untouched.

"When we thought my mother was dying, she had only one request." Sebastian remembered his mother lying on the hospital bed, pale and fragile. She had struggled to speak and he knew this favor meant everything to her, even after all these years. "How could I deny her?"

"I know your mother," Omar said with a frown. "She didn't ask for revenge."

"What I'm doing is righting some wrongs," Sebastian argued. "Finding justice."

"Then I have to ask you this." Omar rested his arms on the table and leaned forward. "What threats did you make to Ashley? What did you take from her? And what will she have left when all this is done?"

"You don't have to worry about Ashley. Spoiled heiresses always land on their feet." Sebastian winced. He shouldn't have called her that. Ashley had once lived in a world of excess and privilege, but if she were really a pampered princess, she wouldn't have survived on her own for this long.

"She's no spoiled heiress," Omar insisted. "Believe me, I'm married to one. Ashley is innocent. She's going to be collateral damage. Just like you were."

Sebastian glared at his friend. Ashley wasn't getting the same treatment that he had received. She lived in luxury and under his protection. "Omar, you don't know what you're talking about."

"I hope not," Omar's eyes were dull with disappointment. "Because I never thought I'd see the day when you became just like Donald Jones."

"I am nothing like that man," he hissed.

"Time will tell," Omar murmured. "Sooner than you think."

It was hours later when Ashley returned to the penthouse apartment with Sebastian. Despite Crystal's inquisitive nature and the painful memories that were dredged up with her pointed questions, Ashley had been determined to end the night on a lighthearted note. She didn't want anyone to know how much her family's action still hurt after all these years.

Sebastian excused himself and went to his office to return a few phone calls. She knew he would be there for a while and she was grateful to have a moment alone. Kicking off her heels, Ashley headed to the swimming pool.

She was too tired to swim. The cold water wasn't going to take away the chill that had seeped into her bones. Ashley paced around the pool as she tried to purge her memories.

"Ashley?" Sebastian's voice cut through her troubled thoughts. "What are you doing here?"

She shrugged. "Just thinking. Don't you have some calls to return?"

"That was hours ago," he said as he strolled toward her.

"Oh." She stopped and stared at the Miami skyline. She had no idea that much time and passed.

"What did Crystal say when you two were alone? Did she upset you?"

Ashley shook her head. "Crystal kept asking the same questions everyone else does. It's nothing I can't handle."

"Her questions stirred up something?"

"I still can't forgive what my parents did to each other," she muttered. "Most of all, I can't forgive myself."

Sebastian frowned. "Why do you need forgiveness?"

Ashley crossed her arms tightly against her. She wanted to remain quiet, but the confession pressed upon her chest. "When I was eighteen I'd had enough of my father's infidelities. I couldn't stand the fact that my mother was unable to see what was going on right under her nose."

"What did you do?" Sebastian asked.

"I told my mother the unvarnished truth." She closed her eyes and remembered her mother's expression. It had been a gradual transformation from disbelief to shock. The pain had etched into her mother's face and Ashley didn't think it would ever disappear. "I had been harsh and I didn't spare her feelings. I was the one who told my mother about his long-standing affair with her best friend."

Sebastian showed no reaction. He wasn't scandalized by her parents' choices or her actions. Most people were and couldn't wait to hear all the dirty details. Instead, he said, "That had to have been the most difficult moment in your life."

"No," she admitted for the first time. "It had been a

relief. I felt we could have a new start. I wanted to end the drama and the fear. I never felt safe while I was growing up. I never knew when another fight would happen."

She wasn't sure why she was telling Sebastian this. Ashley had never shared this secret. She had destroyed her family and no matter how much she stayed on Inez Key and barred herself from the world, she would never find redemption.

But Ashley didn't feel the need to hide this from Sebastian. If anything, she was compelled to share it with him. Her instincts told her that he would understand.

"I didn't care that I betrayed my father," Ashley said, rubbing her hands over her cold arms. "I felt like he had betrayed us a long time ago."

"I take it that your father found out."

"Yes, he shipped me off to college. I should have been grateful to get out of that toxic environment, but instead I retaliated." She had been hurt and out of control. She didn't think she had done anything wrong and her father should have been the one who was punished. "I should have stopped, but instead I told my mother about his other…transgressions. The ones that the tabloids hadn't uncovered. My mother responded by shutting me out of her life."

"Both your parents punished you for telling the truth."

"A month later they were dead," she said as the old grief hit her like a big wave. "Instead of protecting my family, I destroyed it. I caused so much pain."

"You didn't know that would be the end result."

"I knew it wouldn't end quietly. That wasn't their style." She walked past Sebastian, no longer able to face him. She had to get away and find somewhere she could grieve and suffer alone. "People always want to know what triggered the murder-suicide. No one has figured out that I'm the one who set everything into motion."

"Ashley?" he called after her.

She reluctantly turned around, prepared to see the condemnation and disgust in Sebastian's eyes. "What?"

"Whatever happened to the best friend?" he asked. She realized he had already figured out but was looking for confirmation. "The one who had an affair with your father?"

Only he would ask her that. He knew how her mind worked. It should scare her, but she felt he empathized. He knew she wasn't as innocent as she appeared. What he didn't know was that it was the last time she'd confronted and took action instead of running away and hiding.

"I wanted vengeance," she said. "It was wrong of me. I should have let it go, but I couldn't let her get away unscathed. She had pretended to be a loyal friend, but I made sure everyone discovered her true nature. She lost everything that was important to her—her status, her social connections and her husband."

"We're not so different," Sebastian said quietly. "I would have done the same."

Ashley silently walked to Sebastian and rested her head against his shoulder. She sighed as he wrapped his arms around her. She wasn't sure if it had been smart to reveal her darkest secret to Sebastian. He had used her confessions in the past. He had broken his promises.

If he wanted to destroy her completely, nothing could stop him from using this information.

The next morning Sebastian covertly watched Ashley at the breakfast table. Her tousled hair fell over her face like a veil and she wore his bathrobe that overwhelmed her feminine frame. She grasped her mug with both hands and stared into the coffee as if it held all the answers of life.

He knew she loved her morning coffee to the point that it was a sacred ritual, but this was ridiculous. She was hiding from him. Distancing herself.

And Ashley was too quiet for his liking. In the past he would assume the lack of conversation meant she was plotting his demise. Today he suspected she was uncomfortable about sharing her secret with him.

He was offended but he also knew she had a right to feel this way. He didn't have a great track record when it came to Ashley Jones. When she told him about the loan with Raymond Casillas, he had used that information for his benefit. He had also used her sexual attraction to make her his mistress. A broken promise or two, and the possibility that he accidentally got her pregnant....

Sebastian swallowed back an oath. She was probably counting down the minutes until this agreement ended. He needed to show Ashley that he could take care of her in and out of bed. He had to honor his agreement and have her stay on Inez Key.

But would she still want to be with him? Or was she

already distancing herself because there were only a few more days of their arrangement? Was it too late to prove to Ashley that he could be the man she wanted?

Sebastian hated this uncertainty. Most women were content with his attention and his lifestyle. That wasn't enough to hold on to Ashley. For a moment he wished she were pregnant with his child. He had a blistering need to create a lasting connection with this woman.

There was one place he could start. "I have to go on another trip today," Sebastian announced. "I want you to come with me."

Ashley pushed back her hair. "Where are you going this time?"

"Inez Key."

Ashley jerked with surprise. Her fingers shook as she set the coffee mug down with a thud. "You want *me* to go to Inez Key? Why?"

Because he wanted to make her happy. Give her everything she wanted. Find some kind of compromise that could even assuage the guilt that pressed against his chest. "The renovations are almost complete," he said as if that explained everything.

"That was fast," she said with a frown. "How did you manage that?"

"You can accomplish anything when you have money." And he had thrown a great deal of money on the project. Everything had to be perfect in the main house. The grounds had to be exactly as they were twenty-five years ago. Nothing else would do.

"Why do you want me along?"

"You're going to be the caretaker of the island," he said as he took the last sip of his coffee.

Ashley dipped her head. "About that…"

His hand stilled as he listened to her hesitant tone. He thought she would be pleased. Excited to remain on the island. Grateful for the chance to stay.

"I have to decline the offer."

"Why?" She had stayed with him for a month to gain the right to be on the island. Now she was throwing back his offer. "Isn't that what you wanted all along?"

"I needed the island five years ago. It was my haven." Ashley glanced up and met his gaze. "But I'm a different person now and I can't put my life on hold anymore. It's time for me to move on. I can't do that if I'm at Inez Key."

Sebastian struggled with the temptation to argue. He wanted to convince her that the island was the best place for her to stay, but deep down he knew it wasn't true. It was the best thing for *him* if she stayed. She would remain on an isolated island with no single men and always available to him. He liked that idea far too much.

"What are you going to do instead?" he asked gruffly.

Ashley looked away. "I don't know. I'll think of something."

She didn't seem excited about this change in her life. She simply accepted it. But if she didn't want Inez Key anymore, he had no hold on her. Unless he asked her to live with him.

Sebastian's heart pounded hard against his chest. He wanted to extend the invitation, but he wasn't sure what her answer would be. She had rejected him before, and that was before she discovered how he'd double-crossed her. Ashley knew what kind of man he was and she would not willingly choose to share her life with him.

"You should still visit Inez Key with me," he decided. "It would be a good time to collect your things and say goodbye to your friends."

"You're right," Ashley said softly. "I should have one last look and then move on."

Ashley didn't like staying in the antebellum mansion at night. There were too many memories and too many shadows to face in the lonely and quiet house. But tonight was different. The islanders had decorated the beach with torches and flower garlands for her. They danced to the beat of a makeshift drum, sang old pirate songs and drank rum.

The gathering felt more of a coming-of-age celebration than a going-away party. She felt the love and understanding from everyone. She was going to miss them, but she knew they would be thinking of her as she started this new journey.

"Thanks for inviting me to Inez Key," Ashley said to Sebastian as she curled against him while they took the winding staircase to the master suite. "I'm glad I came."

"The islanders are really going to miss you."

"Try not to sound so surprised," she said with an exasperated smile. "Everyone on Inez Key has been like family to me. Clea treated me as an honorary daughter. I'm not sure what she thinks of you." Ashley's smile dipped as she remembered how the older woman had stared intently at Sebastian for most of the party.

"She's angry with me because I'm the reason you're leaving," Sebastian said as he opened the door to the master suite. "She may always see me as the enemy."

Ashley stepped out of Sebastian's arms as she stepped into the master bedroom. She blinked when she noticed the change. The heavy furniture and the four-poster bed that once dominated the room had been replaced. The colorful and modern furniture changed the feel of the room. Erased the oppressive feeling she had whenever she had stepped inside.

"I forgot," Sebastian muttered. "This room had too many memories."

"No, it's okay. I'm right where I want to be." She cupped Sebastian's face with her hands and kissed him. This might be the last chance she had to touch him and lay with him. After her month was up, she no longer had a claim to him.

She broke the kiss and reached for his hand before she silently walked to the bed. She crawled onto the sumptuous bedding and reached for him.

Sebastian didn't seem to be in any rush. He cradled her face and brushed his mouth against hers. His gentleness made Ashley's breath catch in her throat.

He continued to kiss her slowly. Sebastian pressed his mouth against her forehead and her cheeks. His lips grazed the line of her jaw and the curve of her ear. It was as if he was committing her features to memory.

"This is how I would have made love to you the first time," he said as he dragged the thin shoulder straps of her dress down her arms. "If I had known you were a virgin."

"Our first night was special. Perfect," she insisted as she tilted her head back and arched her neck, silently encouraging him to continue. "I don't need a do-over."

"I scared you off," he reminded her as he kissed a trail down her throat.

"I scared myself," she corrected breathlessly as her pulse skipped a beat. "It was too much, too intense. I'd never felt that way before."

"You wanted to hide," he said as he reverently peeled her flirty sundress from her body. "That's why you had rejected my offer."

"It was stupid of me," she admitted as she dragged the buttons free from his shirt. She leaned forward and pressed her mouth against the warm, golden-brown skin she had just revealed. "I didn't mean to come across as a coldhearted bitch."

"What if I made that offer now?" Sebastian's tone was casual, but she sensed he was not asking lightly. "How would you respond?"

Her heart lurched. "That depends," she said huskily. "What is the offer?"

Sebastian shrugged off his shirt and lowered her onto the mattress. He stood before her, proud and male. "Come back to Miami with me."

For how long? And in what role? The questions burned on her tongue but she remained silent. Would she be his occasional hostess or his arm candy? Would she be his hostess or his baby mama?

Ashley wanted to accept his offer immediately and

not look too closely. Refuse to negotiate and dismiss any reservations. She loved him with a ferocity that bordered on obsession. She now understood why her mother had risked everything to be with the man that she loved. The only difference was that Ashley had chosen a good man. A man who would treat her with respect and adoration.

"Well?" Sebastian asked impatiently.

Ashley bit her lip. She wasn't sure whether he was suggesting this because he thought she was pregnant. He had asked her every morning and it didn't help that her period was late. Was he making a strategic move or was this invitation from the heart?

She stretched slowly against the mattress and watched Sebastian's features tighten with lust. "No incentives this time, Sebastian?" she teased.

"I don't have anything you need," he said as he hooked his large fingers underneath the trim of her panties and slowly dragged the scrap of silk down her trembling legs.

She swiped her tongue along her bottom lip. "Don't be too sure about that."

"Tell me what you want," he encouraged softly. "Ask for anything and I will give it to you."

She wanted his love. Ashley knew she should look away before her eyes revealed the truth, but she was ensnared by his hot gaze. She wanted more than his attention or his heart. She wanted everything Sebastian Cruz had to offer. She wished to be part of his life, his future and his very soul.

"You." Her voice croaked as the emotions gripped her chest. "I want you and don't hold anything back."

"And you shall have it," Sebastian said as he crawled onto the bed and hovered above her. His strong arms on either side of her head as his hands pinned her wavy hair. She couldn't move if she'd wanted to.

Sebastian crushed her lips with his mouth before he licked and kissed his way down her chest. He captured her tight nipple with his teeth and teased her with his tongue until the sensations rippled under her skin.

Ashley twisted underneath him as he caressed and laved his tongue against her flat stomach. She bunched the bedsheets in her fists. Her legs shook with anticipation when he cupped her sex with a possessive hand.

Sebastian held her gaze as he stroked the folds of her sex. Her skin grew flush and her breathing deserted her as he rocked her hips. He placed his mouth against the heart of her. Ashley moaned as her core clenched. She went wild under his tongue as he savored the taste of her.

Her climax was swift and brutal. Ashley went limp as her heart raced. She heard Sebastian remove his clothes and she slowly opened her eyes. Sebastian stood at the side of the bed, gloriously naked as he rolled on a condom.

He didn't say anything as he parted her legs with forceful hands before he settled between her thighs. She watched the primitive emotions flickering across his harsh face as he surged into her.

Ashley's gasp mingled with Sebastian's low groan. She rolled her hips as he began to thrust. It was a slow and steady rhythm that was designed to make her lose her mind.

Her flesh gripped him tightly as he surged in deeper. Ashley wanted more. Wanted this to last forever. She wanted Sebastian forever.

"I love you." The words tumbled out of her mouth in an agonized whisper.

Sebastian went still. Ashley closed her eyes and turned her head away. She hadn't planned to reveal her final secret to him.

Sebastian drove into her. His rhythm grew faster. Harder. She didn't dare look at him. Did he feel triumphant or annoyed? Was he amused or irritated by her spontaneous words?

The bed shook with each demanding thrust. It was as if he was branding her with his touch and making the most intimate claim. Another climax—harder and hotter—took her by surprise. She cried out just as Sebastian found his release.

He collapsed on top of her and she welcomed the weight of his sweat-slick body. There was no doubt anymore, she decided as she gulped in air. She belonged to Sebastian Cruz forever.

CHAPTER TEN

THE NEXT MORNING Ashley stood by the double doors that led to the balcony. It was a perfect day at Inez Key; hot with very little humidity. The ocean was calm and a vivid blue. The tropical flowers were opening under the brilliant sun.

But her troubled thoughts didn't allow her to enjoy the view. Ashley glanced at the bed behind her. The sheets were rumpled and the pillows had been thrown on the floor at some time during the night. Yet this morning she had woken up alone.

Sebastian was avoiding her because she had told him she was in love with him. Ashley bit her lip as she recalled that moment. What had gotten into her? She was good at hiding her feelings, but she'd lowered her guard last night. She had been compelled to share how she felt.

And Sebastian didn't say anything in return. In fact, he didn't say anything at all.

Ashley rubbed her forehead and leaned against the door frame. It didn't matter. She had said it in the heat of the moment. He wasn't going to take her words seriously.

She saw a movement on the beach and leaned forward. Sebastian was walking on the dock as he spoke on his cell phone. She couldn't hear his conversation but she knew from the smile and the way he dipped his head that he was speaking to his mother.

Sebastian Cruz was an arrogant and powerful playboy, but he was also a family man. She admired how he took care of his family. She thought that kind of man was only found on unrealistic television shows. But she also noticed how Sebastian treated his mother and sisters.

Unlike the playboys she knew, Sebastian respected women. No matter how exasperated he was with his sisters, Sebastian saw them as successful women who brought a valuable contribution to their fields, community and to the family. He listened to his mother's opinions and sought out her advice. He was ready to help the women in his family if they asked, but he never saw them as useless, porcelain dolls.

Ashley watched from her vantage point, knowing he couldn't see her on the shaded balcony. She could study him and memorize his hard angles and wide shoulders. The man was raw male and sexuality even in his wrinkled cotton shirt and low-slung jeans. It was a shame she wasn't carrying his child.

She'd discovered that this morning, and instead of feeling relieved, Ashley had struggled with her disappointment. She hadn't realized how much she'd wanted Sebastian's baby until that moment. Now there was nothing to keep him at her side.

Ashley saw Sebastian disconnect his call as he

walked to the front door. She couldn't see him but she heard him greet Clea.

"Good morning, Mr. Sebastian," the housekeeper said. Her tone was friendly as usual, but Ashley recognized a bubbling excitement underneath the words. "I've been meaning to ask you, but I haven't had a chance to speak to you alone."

"What do you want to know?" Sebastian's voice was low and rough.

"Did you use to live in this house? I would say about twenty-five years ago?"

Ashley jerked back as her heart stopped. What was Clea saying? That the Cruz family had once owned Inez Key? That was ridiculous, surely.

"Yes," Sebastian said with eerie calm, "this used to be my home until Donald Jones stole it from my family."

Ashley's skin went hot and then cold as the bile churned in her stomach. Her father had taken this island from the Cruz family. Ruined them. And for what? He'd had no interest in Inez Key.

"And you stole it back," Clea said dazedly.

The housekeeper's words echoed in her head. Ashley leaned against the wall as her shaky legs threatened to buckle. That was why Sebastian had been so interested in this island. Why he'd refused to accept Inez Key wasn't for sale.

A collage of images slammed through her mind. Sebastian standing at the dock like a conquering leader. The watercolors Sebastian's father had painted. The shadows in his eyes when he looked at the main house. He'd set out to seduce and steal Inez Key from her because her father had stolen it first. It was an eye for an eye.

Ashley inhaled sharply as the fury and pain whipped through her. She tried to breathe, but her chest was constricted. This was why he didn't respond to her declaration of love. Because he had no feelings for her. She was just a pawn in his game of revenge.

How had she got it so wrong?

She had made herself believe that Sebastian was nothing like the men she knew. That he could love and respect a woman. That he was a good man. A man she could trust and share her life with. Because she believed her happiness and safety was his priority. That he wanted what was best for her.

She had ignored her first instinct. Was it his incredible good looks or his overwhelming sexuality that had distracted her? He used her without compunction. She had been a pawn he could easily sacrifice. She had believed what she wanted to believe.

Ashley closed her eyes and turned her head. She wanted to block out the world around her. Pretend that this wasn't happening. Run and never look back.

But there was a simple truth she couldn't ignore: She was no better than her mother.

Linda Valdez wasn't the only woman in this family who made stupid decisions over the men they loved. Donald Jones had not been worthy of her mother's time or tears, but Linda didn't want to see it. Her mother had built a fantasy world, a place where she had finally felt loved and special.

Ashley slowly opened her eyes. She had done the same.

Ashley couldn't speak. It took all of her strength to stand still when her instincts urged her to escape before she lashed out. The walls were closing in on her. The anger—the howling pain—bubbled underneath the surface, threatening to break free. It was going to be ugly and violent.

No, she wouldn't let it. She was not going down the same path as her mother. Ashley curled her hands into fists and dug her nails in her palms. She welcomed the bite, but it didn't take the edge off her fury. Now, more than ever, she needed to be in control.

She had to get out of here. Her legs were unsteady as she walked across the room. She wanted to double over from the pain but kept walking until she found the bag she had packed in the closet.

Her legs felt heavy and she just wanted to fall into a heap and curl in a protective ball. She blinked as her eyes burned with unshed tears. *Don't cry now*, Ashley thought. *Cry when no one can see you or use your weakness against you. Cry when you're alone.*

Alone. She was all alone with no support system. No home. There was no comfort or peace in her life. Sebastian had taken it all away.

Ashley exhaled slowly, but the pain radiated in her body. She knew she had been different from the other women in his life. She questioned how she'd gained his attention, how she'd attracted him, but hadn't wanted to inspect it too closely. She had been too afraid to poke at her good luck in case it fell apart.

Ashley bent to the waist as the agony ripped through her. It had all been an illusion. All of it.

Even the sex. She leaned against her bedroom door as the nausea swept through her. Especially the sex. He had made her feel special and desirable. Powerful and sexy. Sebastian had introduced her to pleasure. Passion. She thought he had felt the same.

Her body burned with humiliation. She wanted the floor to open up and swallow her whole. Ashley quickly grabbed her bag, knowing she only had a few moments to escape.

She was crossing the floor of the master suite when she heard Sebastian's footsteps down the hall. She barely had time to brace herself when the door swung open.

Her heart gave a brutal leap when Sebastian stood in front of her. She felt so small and insignificant next to him, like a peasant standing before an all-powerful emperor.

"Why didn't you tell me?" she asked in a hiss.

Sebastian noticed her stricken expression and the bag clutched in her hand. He glanced at the doors that led to the balcony and immediately assessed the situation. A shadow crossed his harsh features. He closed the door behind him and leaned against it. He didn't speak as he crossed his arms and watched her.

She felt trapped, weak, and had a fierce need to hide it by striking first. She was never more aware of his intimidating height and powerful build than right at this moment. The button-down shirt and faded jeans didn't hide the fact that he was solid muscle. There was no way she could move him.

"You look upset," he drawled.

Did he still think this was a game? Had he no remorse? "What is Inez Key to you?"

He paused. "It was my childhood home."

"And you felt the need to steal it from me? It was my childhood home as well."

"I didn't steal Inez Key," he pointed out calmly, but she saw the anger flash in his eyes. "Your father did."

"What exactly are you accusing him of?" she asked hoarsely. She knew Donald Jones probably did something underhanded. It was how he approached life.

"He won our home in a poker game," Sebastian said. "But he had cheated."

That sounded like dear old Donald, but maybe this was the one time when her father's reputation automatically made him the culprit. "You don't know that. You have no proof."

Sebastian's eyes narrowed. "He bragged about it years later. His friend Casillas confirmed the story."

Ashley wanted to be ill. "Why did he want the island? It doesn't make sense. My father didn't care about property. He rarely used this island."

The anger whipped around Sebastian. "He wanted something else and tried to use the island as a bargaining chip."

"What?" Ashley couldn't shake off the dread. "What did he really want?"

"My mother." His voice was cold and harsh. "Jones said he wouldn't take the island if he could take my mother to bed instead."

The words drew blood like the lash of a whip. She could easily imagine her father trying to make a deal like that. She'd seen him try many times. And he occasionally succeeded. "Is that why you slept with me?" she asked.

"No," he said in a raspy voice. "I took you to bed because I wanted you and I couldn't stop myself."

She wasn't going to believe that. Not anymore. He had already proven that she had no power over him. He didn't stop himself because he wanted to continue playing the game.

"Don't lie to me," she warned. "It was an eye for an eye. My father tried to blackmail your mother into bed. You did the same to me. Only you were successful." Because apparently she had a price.

"My father wasn't going to let Jones touch my mother. She was his wife. The mother of his children. He should have killed that man for suggesting it."

"And I was a spoiled heiress living the life you should have had," she whispered. She gripped her bag until her knuckles turned white. She wanted to get out. She needed to escape before she said too much or crossed the line.

"Put down the bag," Sebastian ordered. "You're not going anywhere."

"I believed every word you said," she said and scoffed at her ignorance. "You said you would look after me if I got pregnant. I actually thought you meant it."

"I still mean it." Sebastian froze and his gaze quickly traveled down the length of her body.

"Don't worry, Sebastian. I'm not pregnant. Or was that part of the plan too?"

He took a step toward her. "I would never do that to an innocent child."

Ashley backed away. She didn't trust herself around Sebastian. She'd already made a few assumptions and poor choices. He had the ability to make her forget her best intentions with one simple touch. Worse, he knew it.

"But you would do it to me because I couldn't possibly be innocent. I'm Donald Jones's daughter, right? I must be punished."

"Let me explain," Sebastian said as he reached for her.

"No! Don't you touch me. You no longer have that right."

He held up his hands. "Listen to me. When we thought my mother was dying, she made a request. If she survived the surgery, she wanted to live out her remaining years on Inez Key."

Ashley remembered Patricia's faraway look when she'd talked about her home. She was remembering Inez Key. It had been lovingly re-created in the watercolors her husband had painted. It was the paradise she had lost.

"Oh, well, that makes all the difference," Ashley said with heavy sarcasm. "Your mother wanted the island. That excuses the fact that you seduced me and stole my home."

"I'm not making any excuses," he said as he watched her reach the door.

"No, you don't think you need to. You were only getting justice, right?"

"What he did—"

"My father stole the island from you. You stole it from me," she said as she swung open the doors and fled down the stairs. She heard Sebastian's footsteps behind her. "My father wanted to humiliate your parents by blackmailing Patricia into bed. You blackmailed me and tried to humiliate me by making me a mistress. My father's action drove you into poverty. Your actions leave me homeless and broke. Have I missed anything?"

"I had no plans for revenge," Sebastian said as he followed her. "My goal was to buy Inez Key and make it my mother's home."

"Oh, you didn't *plan* to repeat history," she said as she marched to the front door. "You *accidentally* fell into the same pattern that my father followed. What a relief! You don't know how *happy* it makes me feel that you are exactly like Donald Jones."

Sebastian glared at her. "I didn't start this twisted game. I finished it."

"Congratulations, Sebastian. You won." She almost choked on the words as she opened the door and crossed the threshold before she slammed the door shut. "I hope it was worth it."

Ashley didn't notice the aggressive lines of steel and glass as she strode into the Cruz Conglomerate headquarters. The impressive lobby and stunning artwork no longer intimidated her. The anger coursing through her body silenced the noise and the crowds of people surrounding her. She didn't care about anything other than saying a few choice words to Sebastian.

She crushed the buff envelope in her hand as she waited impatiently at the reception desk. She wasn't looking forward to seeing Sebastian. It had been a month since she'd left Inez Key and she didn't feel ready.

She still loved the rat bastard. She shook her head in self-disgust. It was a sign that she was definitely her mother's daughter.

Her first instinct had been to ignore the letter he sent. But how could she? She had felt numb for the last few weeks until she had seen his name on the envelope. She had been pathetically pleased that he knew where she lived. That he was still aware of her.

That ended when she read the letter. Her body shook with anger and hurt, confusion and despair. Every dark emotion whipped through her body until she leaned on the wall and slid to the floor.

This was why she'd cut him out of her life. She couldn't go through this pain. She wasn't going to let her unrequited love tear her apart.

The elegant receptionist hung up the phone and gave her a curious look. "Mr. Cruz will see you right away, Miss Jones."

Ashley nodded as the surprise jolted her system. The last time she was here she had been ignored and forgotten. Now she was given immediate access to Sebastian? She hadn't been prepared for that. Ashley glanced at the exit and took a deep breath. She wasn't going to hide from him. Not anymore.

She was here. Ashley was here to see him. Sebastian stood in the center of his office and buttoned his jacket.

His fingers shook and he bunched his hands into fists. This was an opportunity he couldn't squander. His future, his happiness, was riding on the next few minutes.

The door opened and Ashley rushed inside. "What the hell is this?" she asked as she held up the envelope.

He barely noticed his assistant closing the door and leaving them alone. Sebastian greedily stared at Ashley. This time she didn't feel the need to dress up. He was glad. She looked stunning in her black T-shirt, cutoff shorts and sandals. Her hair was a wild mane and her skin carried the scent of sunshine.

He frowned as he saw that Ashley was vibrating with anger. "That is payment for Inez Key," he said. He thought he had explained everything in the letter.

"Why would you give this to me?" Ashley asked, shaking the envelope close to his face. "You got the island because I couldn't pay back the loan."

"I want to pay you my highest offer because I made a mistake. I went after this island even though it wasn't for sale. My actions were legal but unforgiveable," he admitted through gritted teeth.

"And you think throwing money around is going to make it all go away?" she asked, tossing the envelope onto the floor. "Typical. You rich and powerful men are all the same."

Ashley may look sweet and innocent, but she knew just how to hurt him. "Stop comparing me to your father."

She raised her eyebrows. "Oh, is that what this is all about? You're uncomfortable with the idea that you are just like Donald Jones? Refuse to believe it even though you think like him. You act like him. You destroy lives like him. The only difference is that you out–Donald Jones the original."

"The difference is that I regret what I did. It's tearing me up inside, knowing that you hate me. That your opinion of me is so low." He cursed in Spanish and thrust his hand in his hair. *That you loved me once but I destroyed those feelings.*

"And so you send me a check because you feel responsible? Because you think if you throw enough money at me you think I'll forgive you?" Her voice rose. "Don't get me wrong, Sebastian. I could use the money. I'm flat broke and I don't know if I can make rent next month. But I won't take a penny from you. You think this will absolve what you did? It won't."

"I know that. I can't erase what I did." Sebastian would never forget the hurt in Ashley's eyes when she realized his original plan. He wanted to be a hero in her eyes. He wanted her to look at him in wonder and admiration the way she used to. "The only thing I can do is repair the damage and make amends."

"It's too late."

"I refuse to believe that," he said as the hope died a little inside him. "I want what we had and I am willing to do whatever is necessary to make it happen. Tell me what you need from me. What can I do to regain your trust?"

She glanced up and met his gaze. "There is nothing you can do."

Sebastian felt as if his last chance was disintegrating in his hands. He didn't know what to do and the panic clawed at him. If she gave him a mission, he could earn her trust. But she didn't want anything from him.

"Stay with me," he urged. His request was pathetically simple. He couldn't dazzle her with his wealth and connections. "Give me a chance."

She shook her head. "You don't have to make this offer. I'm not pregnant."

"That's not what I'm asking." Sebastian tasted fear. This reunion wasn't going the way he had envisioned. He was losing her. If she didn't want to be with him, he had nothing to use as leverage. She wasn't interested in his money or power. Those were disadvantages in her eyes. All he could give her was himself. It wasn't enough, but it was a start.

"I need you," he said quietly. "You left this giant hole in my life. I can't sleep. I can't concentrate. All I do is think of you."

Ashley looked away. "You'll get over it."

"I don't want to," he said harshly. "I knew you would be my downfall the moment we met. I didn't care. Nothing mattered but you."

"Getting the island back mattered," she said as the tears shimmered in her eyes. "You used me and betrayed my trust. You planned to cut me out with nothing because that is what my father did to your family. I was just part of your revenge. You would have tossed me to the wolves if you hadn't been attracted to me."

"That's not true! I love you, Ashley."

"Stop playing games with me," Ashley said in a broken whisper. She took a step back and he grabbed her hand. He wasn't going to let her go again.

"You don't have to forgive me at this moment." It hurt that she didn't believe him, but he was willing to work hard at regaining her love and her trust. "Just be with me and I'll prove my love to you every day."

She looked down at their joined hands. Sebastian took it as a good sign that she didn't let go. "I want to but I can't go through this again," she whispered.

He knew how much it cost her to say those words. She risked so much. Maybe even more than when she had declared her love. She still may have feelings for him, that she was willing for another chance. "I want to be the man you need. I want you to believe in me. In us."

The tears started to fall down her cheeks. "I want that, too."

"Stay with me, Ashley," he urged her as his heart pounded fiercely. "I will give you everything you need. Everything you want."

"Stay as what?" she asked as she stepped closer and pressed her hand against his chest. "Your lover? Your mistress?"

"I'm going to make you my wife very soon."

Ashley tugged his tie. "You have to ask first."

"I will," he promised as he covered her mouth with his. "And I'll keep asking until you say yes."

Five years later

Ashley heard the incessant chirping of the nighthawks as she stepped out onto the patio. It had been weeks since she and Sebastian had visited Inez Key. Every time she stepped on the wooden dock, she was struck by how much the island had changed and how much it remained the same.

Sebastian had painstakingly restored the main house, adding a few touches to accommodate his mother's age and mobility. The antebellum house was no longer stark and silent. It was always filled with the shrieking laughter of children and the waft of spices in the big kitchen as everyone had a hand in cooking for the large family dinners.

But this dinner was different, Ashley decided as she caught Sebastian's eye and slowly walked to him. The sky was streaked with orange and red and the birthday candles flickered on the cake she held.

The guests at the long table clapped and cheered when they saw her. She smiled when they began to sing "Happy Birthday." She walked barefoot as the ocean breeze pulled at her casual sundress.

Everyone on Inez Key was there to celebrate. The main house was festooned with streamers, bunting and balloons. The bright colors and loud music reflected the festive spirit of the day. The islanders and the Cruz family mingled at the party that had started early in the day and showed no signs of fading.

Ashley glanced at her mother-in-law. She knew it had been a long and emotional day for Patricia. The older woman, dressed in a vibrant red, was dabbing her eyes with one hand while holding Ashley's infant daughter with the other. Patricia continued to fulfill the wish she'd made almost thirty years ago. She was home surrounded by her family.

Ashley carefully set the cake down in front of Sebastian as he held their boisterous three-year-old twin boys in each arm. She felt his heated gaze on her as the guests sang the last verse.

"Happy birthday, Sebastian," she murmured as she scooped up one of the boys who tried to lunge for the cake. "Make a wish."

"I have everything I want, *mi vida*."

"Ask for anything," she encouraged her husband, "and I'll make it happen."

Ashley saw the devilish tilt of his mouth as the desire flared in his eyes. Anticipation licked through her veins as she watched Sebastian blow out the candles.

As the guests clapped, Ashley saw Sebastian's satisfied smile at the blown-out candles. The curiosity got the better of her. "What did you ask for?"

"If I tell you, it won't come true," he teased. "But this is going to be one birthday wish I'll never forget."

* * * * *

COMING NEXT MONTH FROM
HARLEQUIN *Presents®*

Available January 21, 2014

#3209 A BARGAIN WITH THE ENEMY
The Devilish D'Angelos
Carole Mortimer

International tycoon Gabriel D'Angelo is haunted by the unforgiving eyes that once stared at him across a crowded courtroom. Now the enticing Bryn Jones is back, and this time he'll ensure she plays by *his* rules to get what she wants....

#3210 SHAMED IN THE SANDS
Desert Men of Qurhah
Sharon Kendrick

Bound by a life of restrictions and rules, Princess Leila is desperate for freedom—and Gabe Steel holds the key. Enthralled by her intoxicating touch, Gabe doesn't realize her royal connection...or the lengths he'll have to go to protect her from shame!

#3211 WHEN FALCONE'S WORLD STOPS TURNING
Blood Brothers
Abby Green

Rafaele Falcone may have walked away from her years before, and his sexy Italian accent might still send shivers down her spine, but Samantha Rourke is in the driver's seat this time...with the power to change everything for the ruthless tycoon.

#3212 SECURING THE GREEK'S LEGACY
Julia James

To secure his family's empire, Anatole Telonides must get the beautiful Lyn Brandon to agree to his command...but Lyn is more than the shrinking violet she seems. Her steely resistance entices him to make the ultimate sacrifice—marriage!

HPCNM0114RA

#3213 A SECRET UNTIL NOW
One Night With Consequences
Kim Lawrence
Seeing Angel Urquart brings memories flooding back to
Alex Arlov, stirring up a forgotten hunger. Alex doesn't see why
they can't indulge in one more blazing night together, but Angel
has a secret that will turn their lives upside down....

#3214 SEDUCTION NEVER LIES
Sara Craven
Millionaire Jago is determined to uncover the identity of the
mysterious temptress who trespassed on his property...and to
satisfy the craving she's awakened in him. But seducing Tavi
proves harder than expected—now it's time to up the ante!

#3215 A DEBT PAID IN PASSION
Dani Collins
She may have escaped a prison sentence, but Sirena Abbott
knows she'll be shackled to Raoul Zesiger by more than just the
past. He's determined to recover the debt she owes him...but what
happens when he uncovers the truth behind her theft?

#3216 AN EXQUISITE CHALLENGE
Jennifer Hayward
Alexandra Anderson is the *only* woman who can help with wine
magnate Gabe De Campo's highly anticipated launch event.
But these two are a lethal combination—with so much at stake,
can they resist the powerful attraction between them?

**YOU CAN FIND MORE INFORMATION ON UPCOMING HARLEQUIN® TITLES,
FREE EXCERPTS AND MORE AT WWW.HARLEQUIN.COM.**

HPCNM0114RB

REQUEST YOUR
FREE BOOKS!

2 FREE NOVELS PLUS
2 FREE GIFTS!

YES! Please send me 2 FREE Harlequin Presents® novels and my 2 FREE gifts (gifts are worth about $10). After receiving them, if I don't wish to receive any more books, I can return the shipping statement marked "cancel." If I don't cancel, I will receive 6 brand-new novels every month and be billed just $4.30 per book in the U.S. or $4.99 per book in Canada. That's a saving of at least 14% off the cover price! It's quite a bargain! Shipping and handling is just 50¢ per book in the U.S. and 75¢ per book in Canada.* I understand that accepting the 2 free books and gifts places me under no obligation to buy anything. I can always return a shipment and cancel at any time. Even if I never buy another book, the two free books and gifts are mine to keep forever.

106/306 HDN FVRK

Name _____ (PLEASE PRINT)

Address _____ Apt. #

City _____ State/Prov. _____ Zip/Postal Code

Signature (if under 18, a parent or guardian must sign)

Mail to the **Harlequin® Reader Service:**
IN U.S.A.: P.O. Box 1867, Buffalo, NY 14240-1867
IN CANADA: P.O. Box 609, Fort Erie, Ontario L2A 5X3

**Are you a current subscriber to Harlequin Presents books
and want to receive the larger-print edition?
Call 1-800-873-8635 or visit www.ReaderService.com.**

* Terms and prices subject to change without notice. Prices do not include applicable taxes. Sales tax applicable in N.Y. Canadian residents will be charged applicable taxes. Offer not valid in Quebec. This offer is limited to one order per household. Not valid for current subscribers to Harlequin Presents books. All orders subject to credit approval. Credit or debit balances in a customer's account(s) may be offset by any other outstanding balance owed by or to the customer. Please allow 4 to 6 weeks for delivery. Offer available while quantities last.

Your Privacy—The Harlequin® Reader Service is committed to protecting your privacy. Our Privacy Policy is available online at www.ReaderService.com or upon request from the Harlequin Reader Service.

We make a portion of our mailing list available to reputable third parties that offer products we believe may interest you. If you prefer that we not exchange your name with third parties, or if you wish to clarify or modify your communication preferences, please visit us at www.ReaderService.com/consumerchoice or write to us at Harlequin Reader Service Preference Service, P.O. Box 9062, Buffalo, NY 14269. Include your complete name and address.

HP13

"TELL ME YOU don't want me to kiss you, that you don't want that as much as I do, and I won't ask you again," he rasped harshly.

Her throat moved as she swallowed convulsively. "I can't do that," she acknowledged achingly, her voice carrying a desperate sob.

"You want me to make that decision for both of us, is that it?" he bit out harshly.

Bryn was no longer sure what she wanted!

Well…she was, but what she wanted—to kiss and to be kissed by Gabriel—was what she shouldn't want.

He was a D'Angelo, for goodness' sake. And no matter how charming and entertaining he had been this evening, underneath all that charm he was still the cold and ruthless Gabriel D'Angelo from all those years ago. To allow herself—to *want*—to kiss and be kissed by that man, went against every instinct of loyalty she had, as well as every shred of self-preservation she possessed.

Except…she couldn't escape the fact that the man she had met earlier today, the man she had just spent the evening with—the same man who made her pulse race and caused her body to be so achingly aware of everything about him—

wasn't in the least cold or ruthless, but was instead hot and seductive. *That* man she desperately wanted and longed to kiss.

Which was utter madness, when she knew exactly how Gabriel would react if he knew who she really was.

"Please let me, Bryn."

She couldn't breathe as she looked up at Gabriel, unable to make a move to stop him as his hands moved up to cup her cheeks and lift her face to his, feeling herself drowning, becoming totally lost, in the dark and enticingly warm depths of his piercing brown eyes as his mouth slowly descended toward hers.

* * *

Can fledgling artist Bryn Jones make a deal with the devil and survive, or will the fire that burns between her and the sinfully sexy gallery owner Gabriel D'Angelo engulf them both?

Find out in February 2014, wherever books and ebooks are sold.

HPEXP0114-1

"Was it a punishment, Sam? Hmm?" He answered himself. "Punishment for my being finished with you? For not wanting more? For letting you go? For not wanting to have a baby because that's not what our relationship was about?"

Rafaele couldn't stop the demon inside him.

"I think the problem is that you fell for me and you were angry because I didn't fall for you, so you decided to punish me. It's so obvious...."

Sam closed the distance between them, her hand lifted and she hit Rafaele across the face before she even registered the impulse to do so. She realised in the sickeningly taut silence afterward that she'd reacted because he'd spoken her worst fears out loud. Here in this awful, stark, echoey room.

With a guttural curse, and his cheek flaring red where Sam had hit him, Rafaele hauled her into his arms and his mouth was on hers. He was kissing her angrily, roughly.

It took a second for Sam to get over the shock, but what happened next wasn't the reaction she would have chosen if she'd had half a brain cell still working. Her reaction came from her treacherous body and overrode her brain completely.

She started kissing him back, matching his anger with her

own. For exposing her. For saying those words out loud. For making her feel even more ashamed and confused. For being *here*. For making her want him. For making her remember. For kissing her just to dominate her and prove how much she still wanted him.

Her hands were clutching Rafaele's jacket. All she could taste was passion, and it sent her senses spiraling out of all control. Rafaele's hands were on her arms, and tears pricked behind Sam's eyelids at the tumult of desire mixed with frustration.

She opened her eyes to see swirling green oceans. Rafaele pulled away jerkily and Sam could hear nothing but the thunder of her own heartbeat and her ragged breathing. She was still clutching his jacket, so she let go, her hands shaking.

* * *

Just what will the ruthless Rafaele do to get revenge on the woman who kept him from his son?

*Find out in February 2014,
wherever books and ebooks are sold.*

HPEXP0114-2